Other books by Duane Bradley

ENGINEERS DID IT!

MYSTERY AT THE SHOALS

TIME FOR YOU: HOW MAN MEASURES TIME

By Duane Bradley and Eugene Lord

HERE'S HOW IT WORKS

OUR WORLD OF SCIENCE

MEETING
WITH
A STRANGER

MEETING

WITH

A STRANGER

~~~~~~

by DUANE BRADLEY

ILLUSTRATED BY E. HARPER JOHNSON

J. B. LIPPINCOTT COMPANY

Philadelphia and New York

"Cut down the cantuffa in the four quarters of the world, for I know not where I am going."

—ANCIENT ETHIOPIAN IMPERIAL DECREE

THIS BOOK is dedicated, with affection and gratitude, to two people whose generous aid and advice helped make it accurate, and whose lives help make it true: Dr. Edith Lord of our State Department, and Ato Tekle Ab Kassaye of Ethiopia.

Dr. Lord served for four years as Education Advisor in the Ethiopian-United States Cooperative Education Program in Ethiopia. Ato Tekle Ab is a brilliant and charming young Ethiopian writer whose pride in the cultural inheritance of his country is surpassed only by his hopes for its future.

Though of different races, backgrounds, languages and nationalities, they share one priceless trait—to know either of them is to respect the country he represents, and to know both of them is to have higher hopes for the world in which we live.

To Edith and Tek, then, whose strangers all are friends.

DUANE BRADLEY
July 23, 1963

CONTENTS

1

THE WHITE POWDER

OF THE

FERANGI

"AND here," said his uncle, "is the school."

Teffera looked at the large building, so square and red and strange, with big shining clear windows. He did not think he liked it.

"You will come here every day," his uncle went on, "and learn all of the things you need to know."

It would not be polite to disagree with his uncle, but Teffera did not believe the school could teach him much about sheep.

"Perhaps my father will want me to stay at the farm," he said softly. "I can take care of the sheep for him until his eyes are better."

His uncle laughed sharply, with a sound that cut through the clear air.

"The sheep are sick," he said. "They are thin and poor, and the lambs are weak. If the sheep die, and your father's eyes do not get better, what will happen then?"

His uncle did not wait for him to answer, but took a breath and went on talking.

"No, it will be better for you to go to school so that in a few years you can get a good job. Then you can make a home for your parents here in town, and take care of them. If I had a son, that is what I would want him to do."

Teffera nodded and said nothing, because it would make no difference. Tomorrow his uncle would take him back to the farm and talk to his father, and he would do as they said.

It would be good to get back to the farm. Three months ago he had left it, at the time the rains began, but he could not remember much about that.

He had been driving the donkey, bringing wood in to the farm, when the donkey had been frightened and had bolted. His great fear he could remember, and the sudden crash, then nothing. The next time he had opened his eyes he had been in a white room with a strange woman near him, and his head and back shot through with pain.

Later he had been told that the place was a clinic and over and over again he heard how fortunate he was to have been brought there. His uncle, who had not visited the family farm for so many years, had been called and had come with his wife to visit him.

"This, too, is an old belief that we will outgrow," he had said, "When someone is in the clinic, as you are, it is not necessary for his whole family to stay with him to see that he is well cared for. These doctors and nurses will heal all of your wounds and make you whole again, but they would do the same even if I were not here."

Nevertheless, Teffera was glad that his parents had called his uncle. It had been comforting to see a family face, even one that was not too familiar, among all the strange ones.

He was too well brought up to argue with any adult, so he had told no one how he hated the clinic. There had been ferangi there with strange red faces and hands, and their voices had been loud and harsh. They had wrapped his head and shoulders in tight cloth, needles had been stuck in him, and he had been given things to swallow. No Ethiopian boy cried, but to himself he could admit that he had swallowed many tears in the darkness where no one could see.

The clinic and the whole big rushing town where his uncle lived were both too busy to care about one person. The streets were crowded, and there was too much noise. Even now, as he and his uncle walked, people pushed against them, and they had to make way for speeding cars and herds of animals.

He would be glad to get back to his uncle's house, where he had been taken after leaving the clinic, although it was strange and uncomfortable. His uncle was proud of it because it had cost a great deal and had many foreign things in it. They even ate foreign food with unfamiliar tools.

Like all boys, Teffera thought many things he did not say. Now he could understand why Uncle Bekele, who had been at the farm so much in former years, came so seldom now, and why his father's voice was strained when he spoke of him. His uncle acted as if he were ashamed of being an Ethiopian and of all the good, familiar things so dear to the rest of the family.

Some of the people they passed spoke to Bekele as if he were a very important man. This made Teffera proud, but it worried him, too. Was it because his uncle was dressed like a ferangi, and the whole world was going mad? Did they think it was better to pretend to be a ferangi instead of being proud of being an Ethiopian?

He could not understand it. Perhaps when his father and uncle talked he could listen carefully and find the answers to his questions.

The evening meal was ready when they got home, and his aunt had made injerra and wett for him because she knew he was homesick. Almost greedily he ate the flat, pancake-like bread

13

with the thick, bright red, delicious sauce. He noticed that his uncle, who usually scorned the dishes of his youth, seemed just as hungry as he.

"Now, Teffera," his uncle said, "we will have a very important guest tonight. His name is Mr. Sam Jones, and he is from America."

The words sounded peculiar to Teffera, but he did not want to ask questions.

"You must remember to call him Mr. Jones. Now show me how you will greet him."

Teffera got to his feet obediently.

He bowed low and said, "Welcome, Ato Mister Sam."

Instead of taking his outthrust hand, his uncle doubled over with laughter. "No, no," he said. "You do not know how the foreigners do things. If you were speaking to me, you would call me Ato Bekele Abraham, because that is the right way to say my name. But foreigners have strange ways. Instead of Ato, they say Mister, and they do not use the real name, but the second one. You must say, 'How are you, Mr. Jones?' "

Teffera thought it was all too puzzling. His own name was Teffera Paulos, and when he was grown he could be called Ato Teffera. Paulos was his father's name, and to call him Ato Paulos would sound as if he were not a person in his own right. Perhaps it was as his father said, that foreigners were without proper pride and manners.

He was curious, though, to see a ferangi closely and listen to him talk. His uncle would allow him to sit quietly in a corner of the room and hear all that was said, and he would have much to think about.

The loud barking of the household dogs announced the arrival of a taxi, and quick loud footsteps approached the front door. The sharp noise of pounding on the door made Teffera start. Could it be Mr. Sam Jones, and was he angry about something?

His uncle Bekele did not seem alarmed, but went to the door

and opened it, a bright smile on his face.

"How are you?" he asked. "Please come in. We are happy to see you."

Teffera watched as they shook hands, instead of bowing deeply to each other as was proper. How shocked his father would be if he could see it.

His uncle turned to him. "Mr. Jones," he said, "this is my nephew, Teffera. Teffera this is Mr. Jones. Teffera is the son of my brother in the country, who raises sheep."

Teffera was shocked to feel his hand gripped violently, squeezed, and pumped vigorously up and down. It was not a warm and courteous greeting, but more as if the stranger were trying to prove how strong he was.

His astonishment grew as Mr. Sam Jones took off his coat, tossed it carelessly to one side, and sprawled out comfortably in a chair.

"Do you mind if I relax?" he asked. "It's been a rough day." He was speaking Amharic, but not as Teffera had ever heard it spoken before. To his amazement, Mr. Sam Jones turned to him.

"Well, and how are you, young man? You raise sheep, eh? Having trouble with them?"

How did one speak to a grown man who acted so strangely? It was not proper to undress in front of others, to act as if one were alone and about to go to sleep. However, his uncle was watching, and he must do the best he could. He kept his voice low and clear so that his emotions would not be noticed.

"Oh, no, thank you very much. They are well."

His uncle shrugged his shoulders and smiled.

"You see how our children are taught," he said. "The sheep are not at all well, but are sick. They are poor and thin, and many of the lambs die, but Teffera has been taught that it is not polite to say something unpleasant."

Mr. Jones slapped Teffera on the shoulder. "That's not a bad idea, son. In our country we say, 'If you can't say something good, don't say anything at all,' but it depends on circumstances. Now tell me about your sheep, and maybe I can help."

Teffera looked at his uncle in bewilderment. In spite of all the noise Mr. Jones made, and his strange manners, he seemed friendly. But how could he talk to him? It was his role to sit quietly and listen, not to speak in the presence of adults.

His uncle spoke. "You must do as he says, Teffera. Mr. Jones has come from a land very far away because he is interested in our country and wants to help us. In his country, children are not taught as they are here, so he will not think you rude if you speak to him. I asked him here tonight because I think he can help make your sheep well, but you must tell him all about them so he will know what kind of sickness they have."

It was almost impossible for Teffera to begin. The only people to whom he could speak long and freely were boys of his own age. Then he had a clever idea—he pretended that the odd Mr. Jones was a boy. He did not forget, however, to keep his head slightly bowed and his eyes turned away from Mr. Jones's face.

Even then it took many questions, and he had to think a great deal before he could explain about the sheep. There was no purpose to it, in any case, because the sickness of the sheep was the will of God. He had tended them carefully, had taken them to the best pastures, and had guarded them from hyenas, but they were still sick. If he had been at fault, he could do better, but he had not been at fault.

"It is because of Mascal," he said slowly. "We did not make a big feast last year because we had lost too many sheep. My grandfather says that we must praise God whether it is a good year or a poor year, and we did not, and now the sheep are sick."

"That may well be," agreed Mr. Jones, "but how are the sheep sick? What do they do?"

Little by little Teffera scanned his memory of the sheep and told him. The many questions Mr. Jones asked made him uncomfortable, but he did as his uncle wished and tried to answer

17

all of them. When it was over he was very tired and glad to have Mr. Jones get up to leave.

Mr. Jones paused at the door. "I know what the problem is," he said. "I'll mail you some stuff to give them. It will be a white powder to put in their feed. It won't solve all of your problems, but it will help."

Teffera kept a polite smile on his face, even as he said goodnight to his uncle, but it slipped away as soon as he was alone.

Not for anything would he give a strange white powder to his precious sheep. Even though this was the first time he had talked to a ferangi, he knew much that was bad about them.

Long, long ago, when his grandfather was very young, Ethiopia had fought ferangis who tried to take over the country. At Adowa his people had defeated the enemy, and sent them on their way.

Later than that, when his father was a boy, ferangis had come to the country again, pretending to be friends. Then they had turned on Ethiopia, and brought five years of hardship and trouble to the country. These five years of guerilla warfare could never be forgotten, nor, as the ancient elders had ever proclaimed, any ferangi trusted.

"When he sends the white powder," Teffera thought, as he drifted off to sleep, "I will put it in a fire and burn it so that it can do no harm."

2

~~~~~~

THE TIME

OF

BUHE

IT WAS raining heavily when Teffera awoke in the morning, but he did not care. It always rained most in the month of Nahase; if it did not, how could the grass grow to feed the sheep? And if one is going home, the sun shines in the heart.

His uncle and aunt were dressed in their right clothes; his aunt's shemma beautiful with bright embroidery. When they got into the car and began driving in the direction of the farm, Teffera could almost believe that everything that had happened in the last three months had been a bad dream.

For a long time the road was good, and then the car turned off onto a rougher one that was still not too bad. The rain had stopped and clouds raced across the sky high above them. Flowers, damp and gleaming, began to give out their special odors, and the whole high mountain plateau was fresh and sweet.

Teffera feasted his eyes on everything he saw; then curled up in the back seat of the car and went to sleep. It was a long way

to his father's house, and he had not slept well the night before.

The bumping of the car finally awakened him and he sat up, rubbing his eyes and yawning. In a little while he knew where he was, because he had been this far from home once before. The road was not very good, but then it was not often used for cars, just by people walking or on burros.

As they passed a house Teffera saw a sight that made his heart beat fast. Leaning on the fence that surrounded the house were torches—torches ready to be used for Buhe! In his long stay away from home he had forgotten how much time had passed, and that this wonderful time was here.

The car went faster than he could have walked, yet his heart seemed to run ahead of it, eager to see his home and his parents again. Mile after mile passed with maddening slowness, but eventually the road wound down hill and his own village was clearly before him, nestling in the valley.

20

Eucalyptus trees grew around the houses, the tallest clump surrounding the round church, which was bigger than any house. The houses, too, were round, each roofed with tawny thatch, so much prettier than the metal roofs of the houses in the big city.

They left the car and walked down the rough hillside until they reached the courtyard of his own home. At last he was standing on his own land once more!

"Call and tell them that we are here," said his uncle. Teffera raced to obey him.

His father stood at the open door of the house, one hand shading his eyes. A smile lighted his face as he heard Teffera's voice.

The boy bowed low before his father and kissed his feet in greeting. Tears came to his eyes as his father's strong hands pressed his shoulders and the voice he had not heard for so long spoke.

"Welcome home, my son, light of tomorrow!"

Then they were all together again. His mother holding him close, and his father and uncle exchanged the many kisses on the cheek given to close relations.

Teffera was home where he belonged, and the voices of his reunited family were soft in his ears and beautiful, like the song of birds.

"We must eat now," his father said, "because you are tired and hungry after your long trip. Then our neighbors will come to greet you, and we will have a celebration to thank God for His goodness in all that has happened."

The good familiar food was ready on the table, and for the first time Teffera was seated with the others. It was not only because he was now almost a man, but because he had been away for so long. His father broke the first piece of injerra and gave it to Teffera's mother; then everyone began eating at once.

Even before they were finished they heard the voices of their neighbors outside. Teffera was eager to join his friends again and tell them everything that had happened to him in the terrible city.

As soon as his father dismissed him he went outside and was immediately surrounded by the boys of the village. They listened quietly as he talked, but it was clear they did not believe everything he told them. The story of the strange ferangi, Mr. Sam Jones, was greeted with derision.

"So a ferangi, an Americour, talked to you, eh? Were you afraid? Those people smile at you and really make you feel that you are grown up, don't they? Did he get you to say something foolish?"

Teffera understood the way his friends felt, but he shook his head solemnly. "I did not believe all that he said," he boasted. "I was very clever and said nothing foolish to him."

Retta, who was his best friend, called him to one side. "Everyone wants to play games now, but later on I will tell you something. You and I will lead the group for Buhe, and you must come with me to get my torches, so we can be alone for a while."

"Let's play debebkosh," someone said, and the others agreed. "Teffera must be the Seeker, and Retta can be the Chief."

Retta seated himself in a spot where he could see everyone clearly: Teffera knelt in front of him. He put his head in his friend's lap and shut his eyes tightly. All around him he could hear whispering and giggling as the others ran to hide.

When he thought they had all had plenty of time, he spoke "Kukululu?" He trilled the word in his throat as he said it, because it was an imitation of the rooster crowing, to announce that the sun has risen.

Quickly Retta answered, "Al-ne-gam." This meant it was still not time to search. Three times they exchanged the centuries-old signals, until finally Retta shouted, "Nega!" and Teffera was free to search for the hiders.

He got to his feet and began to look. Suddenly a ten-year-old ran out from behind a bush and darted toward Retta. Teffera chased him, but the younger boy was too fast and reached his goal before he could be touched.

Boy after boy darted out of his hiding place and raced to be safe.

Teffera finally caught one, who then had to play the role of Seeker. In the next game, Teffera went to hide with the others.

All afternoon they played. Teffera could feel his unused muscles becoming strong and supple again, and his spirits rising. When everyone was thoroughly tired, a few wanted to play something quieter, but Teffera and Retta went off by themselves.

"My torches this year are better than ever before," Retta told him. "My father made you a good whip, because you have been gone for so long, and he thought your father might not have time."

Teffera knew that his friend was too polite to say that his father's eyes were too bad for him to see clearly enough to make a good whip, but he was happy that he could have one.

He examined it carefully at Retta's house and saw what a marvelous job it was. The long strands of fiber were carefully braided together and fastened securely to the strong pliant handle. He tested it and the fibers snapped loudly, making a sharp noise that delighted his heart.

"I will not forget to thank your father," he said. "I think this is the best whip I have ever seen." This was not quite true, because his own father had once made him fine ones, but it was the only way he knew to say how grateful he was.

When they returned to his house his torches were ready, and the other boys were gathered, eager to begin their trek through the village.

Retta as always was chosen the leader because he knew the Buhe songs so well and had such a good voice. Teffera was made treasurer, and his mother gave him a big basket to carry the gifts of bread. The sun was setting; the long, mysterious shadows and the cries of the hyenas back in the hills sent a happy shiver down Teffera's spine.

Almost since he could remember, he had celebrated Buhe with the other boys of the village, and soon he would be too old. Retta raised his voice in one of their favorite songs. After he had sung the first part the others sang it together.

With torches to light their way, and the light from the different houses to guide them, they visited the home of each of their neighbors in turn, snapping their whips and singing.

As they came near a gate, Retta sang sweetly.

"The mistress should rise and light the lamp and the master should rise and look for the bread."

At each house they were given loaves of the special bread of Buhe, which Teffera put into his basket. To give thanks for the gift, they sang, "He who insults my mistress, let him have the odor of a bedbug, and he who insults my master, let him itch."

It was understood that the boys might play tricks on anyone who refused to give them bread, but this was a good village and no one was so selfish. When each house had been visited Teffera's basket was full and the boys' voices were hoarse from so much singing.

24

It was getting late and time for the bonfire, which they had decided would be in front of Teffera's house, to do him honor. Carefully they piled the torches together, everyone having his say as to how they should be arranged to make the biggest fire.

As the flame burned higher and higher, the boys shouted with joy. Retta began another song and they all joined in, their voices happy in the dark night.

As they sang, they snapped their whips and ate the bread, rejoicing in the celebration which was for the glory of God, and the pleasure of boys.

Teffera was so happy and so tired he had forgotten that Retta had something important to tell him until he heard his voice just beside him.

"Come over here," Retta said, "where we can be alone."

The two friends sat down in the shadows away from the fire and Teffera listened while Retta told him the strange story.

"Some ferangis have come to the village of Sheleko," said Retta, "and I heard my father tell his friends what they did to the sheep. They cut the hair from some of them, and stuck needles into some of them, and killed some of them. My father says that the ferangis wish to take over our country again, but they know we are too strong to beat in battle, so they want to kill all of our sheep instead. Then when we have no sheep we will starve, so they can have our country for themselves."

Teffera listened fearfully as his friend told him more of the terrible things the ferangis were doing. He remembered the round, red, smiling face of Mr. Sam Jones, and wondered how anyone could seem so friendly and yet be so evil.

"Why don't they stay in their own country," he asked, "and leave us alone?"

"They say they have come to help us," said Retta. "They say that their own country is very big and rich and strong, and that their people are very wise. They want to teach us and show us many things so we can be like them."

Mr. Sam Jones's face floated before Teffera's eyes and he shook his head. He remembered something he had heard his father say.

" 'It is easy to tell lies about a far country,' " he quoted. "If their country is so wonderful, why have they left it to come here?"

"And why should we want to be like them?" asked Retta. "There is nothing about us that is the same. I wish they would all go away and leave us alone."

Teffera knew that if he were not so nearly a man he would be very frightened. He shivered a little, sitting in the warm darkness and thinking of the terrors that had now come so close.

3

THE KAGNAZMATCH

ABRAHAM

SPEAKS

THE next day there was a feeling of excitement in the house and the courtyard around it. Teffera's mother and the servant girl were busy cooking; his father paced restlessly up and down, talking to Bekele. Teffera tried to be everywhere at once so he could be helpful, and still hear what was being said.

His grandfather was coming—that much he knew, and his heart leaped high. Surely there was not a more wonderful man, except for his father, in all of Ethiopia! Tall and straight and handsome, made more dignified and impressive by his sixty years, the courage that had made him a mighty hunter in his youth could be seen in every glance of his dark eyes.

He would know a way to defeat the ferangi, and perhaps even the right medicine to cure the eyes of Teffera's father. Then all would be well again, and Teffera could forget his worries.

The beating of drums and the deep pleasant sounds of men's voices came to his ears. He rushed to the gate of the courtyard.

Sure enough, it was his grandfather, the great Kagnazmatch Abraham Kidane. Sitting proudly erect in his silver-mounted saddle, his spotless white shemma gleaming under his brilliantly embroidered blue cape, his eyes flashing and his face smiling with joy, he was every inch a king among ordinary men, and those men the proudest people on earth.

Teffera ran to greet him and bowed low to the ground. Then he stood quietly to one side until it was time for him to be noticed.

The women of the household brought out food and drink, and there was much loving, happy talk, as there is with people who do not see each other often but feel very close. In the afternoon, the men of the family sat down together, and it was clear that weighty matters were to be discussed. To his amazement, Teffera heard his own name called.

"You will join us, Teffera. Soon you will be a man, and what concerns the family concerns you," his grandfather said.

When they were seated, Kagnazmatch Abraham turned to his son, Teffera's father. "And how are your eyes, my son?"

Paulos faced him squarely, his own face as strong and as brave as his father's, but torn with trouble and sorrow. "I cannot lie to you. Every evening I have put the leaves the wogesha gave me on them, and every morning they are no better."

Kagnazmatch Abraham nodded slowly. "And if they are no better, my son, are they worse?"

The words seemed bitter on Paulos's tongue. "Every day they are worse," he said. "At first it was as if the sun was hiding behind a thin cloud, but each day the cloud gets darker, and now it is almost as if the night is upon me."

"And what do you plan to do?"

Paulos shook his head in despair. "I do not know. With the help of Teffera and my household, we are able to keep the farm going. I have thought that Teffera is almost a man and will soon be able to take my place. Bekele tells me that is wrong."

"And what is it that you say, Bekele?"

Bekele leaned forward, his eyes shining. "I say that misfortune can be outwitted. It is one thing to be brave and to bear troubles patiently, but sometimes that is the fool's way. The wise man finds a new path when the old one is washed away."

He stood up, so carried away with his ideas that he could not sit still. "For many years I have tried to tell Paulos that a new day has come to our country. Teffera should be a part of that new day, and not live buried in the past. I say that he should come to live with me in the town and go to a school. He will be taught many things, and when he is finished he can get a job in the town and make a home for his parents."

"What kind of job would that be?"

"It could be many different things. He could work in an office or teach school or choose what he liked."

Kagnazmatch Abraham's eyes flashed like lightning in a summer storm. "And in these jobs," he asked abruptly, "would he work with the ferangis?"

Bekele bowed his head before his father's gaze. "Perhaps," he admitted. "Many Ethiopians do."

"Reeds bend in the wind," said his father, "but not trees. Is it good that some of our people are following ferangi ways? Is it not true that the townsmen are forgetting our history and what we are, and trying to be like foreigners?" His voice softened. "Do not fear to speak to me honestly and freely, Bekele. I am no fool, and I know that things are changing in our country. We who are alive today cannot live yesterday over again. But this must not keep us from using our wisdom to solve our problems."

Bekele made a sudden gesture toward Teffera. "Come here," he said, and drew the boy close to his grandfather. "Take off your shemma and shirt," he ordered.

Teffera did as he was told, uncertain what was going to happen.

Bekele put his hands on the boy's shoulders and turned him

carefully around. "Look at him closely, father, and see how strong and well he is. When I took him into town he was cut in many places, and his bones were broken. If the wogesha had tried to heal him, Teffera would be crippled and weak. In the new hospital they knew what to do, and you can hardly tell that he was ever injured."

He released Teffera and motioned for him to put his clothes on.

"I love Ethiopia as much as any man, and I want what is best for her. For thousands of years we have lived on top of our high mountains, considering the rest of the world nothing but a stretch of sand. When the ferangi came, they brought us trouble. Perhaps our memories are too long, and we forget that they also brought us other things.

"Now they tell us that the world is changing. Are we so proud that we cannot believe them? Paulos has chosen to stay here with his land where he can live as our people have always lived. I chose to go to the town and learn what I could of the new wisdom. When Teffera was hurt, it was not the old ways that saved him, but the new. If he stays on the farm he can learn to take the place of Paulos, but why should he tie himself to the past?"

Kagnazmatch Abraham turned to Paulos. "And what do you say to this?"

Paulos shook his head. "I do not like following blindly in the way of the ferangis. It is said that one must eat fish with care. If we try to go ahead too rapidly, we will be swallowing the fish whole, taking the bones with the meat."

Kagnazmatch Abraham put his hands over his eyes for a minute and was silent. "We must remember that our country is beloved of God," he said. "For many centuries all the people of the world called it God's land, and they spoke truly. But because this is true, we must not think that other people are not worthwhile. Since God made them, He must love them, too."

Paulos spoke softly. "But I do not trust them," he said. "I have

31

heard of terrible things they are doing, even now."

"I know. I have heard such stories." Kagnazmatch Abraham looked again at Teffera. "Were they kind to you in the place where they made you well? Did anyone hurt or frighten you?"

All that Teffera could remember was bad, but he wanted to be truthful. No one had spoken harshly to him, no one had hurt him except when they bound his arms and shoulders tightly and stuck needles in him. His uncle had said those things were to make him well. There was no doubt that he was well, and that he had been injured very badly in the accident.

"I did not like it," he said, "but they were not cruel to me."

Kagnazmatch Abraham looked Bekele squarely in the eyes. "Can they do great things in these hospitals? Can they cure ills that our wogesha cannot?"

"Oh, yes. There is no doubt of that."

"And could they cure such a thing as this?" He pointed at the eyes of Paulos, and the room was silent with the shock of what he had said.

Bekele thought a long time before he spoke.

"Yes, father, I believe they could. Perhaps not in the hospital in my town, but certainly in the bigger one in Addis Ababa. I have heard that they almost perform miracles there."

Kagnazmatch Abraham nodded his head.

"It would be a dangerous thing to put oneself in the hands of the ferangis, and no one could tell what might happen. Perhaps they are good as Bekele says, and perhaps they are wicked, as Paulos thinks. Whatever they are, they might cure your eyes for reasons of their own, Paulos. What do you think?"

Teffera could feel that his father was looking at him, and he dared not meet his eyes. At last Paulos spoke.

"A man who cannot see is only half a man. For the last few months Teffera has had most of the care of the sheep, and things are so bad that Bekele wants to take him away from the farm forever. I will go to the hospital in Addis Ababa, but if I do,

Teffera must stay here and be a man in my place while I am gone."

Bekele went quickly to his brother and clasped both of his hands in his.

"You are a brave man, Paulos. You will not regret what you are doing. Teffera will stay here on the farm and care for it, and I will help him."

"But there is one thing," Paulos said clearly. "If I put myself in the hands of the ferangis, it does not mean that I trust in them, or believe in them, or will follow their ways. If they give me back my sight, it will be as if I went into the wild jungle and killed a lion, and brought his skin back with me. I will take what I can get from the ferangis, but I will not become one of them."

4

~~~~~~

CUT DOWN

THE

CANTUFFA

WHEN the village learned that Paulos was going to a hospital in Addis Ababa, there was great excitement. It made Teffera feel important to know that everyone was talking about his family, but he wondered what it would be like to be without a father for a while.

"Wait and see," Retta told him. "When your father is gone, the ferangis will come. They will get our sheep and cut off their wool, and stick needles in them, and all of them will die."

"The other men of the village will be here. My father is not the only man in town."

"No, but he is the one people listen to. Without him to advise us, what will we do?"

Teffera thought of this as he sat on the hillside in the sweet meadow and watched the sheep. His father had a large herd, but it was smaller than the year before. Sheep were never very lively creatures, except when they were lambs, and now they seemed tired out from their sickness. It would be easy for the ferangis to kill them when they were already so weak.

How could he protect them while his father was away? He was not old enough, or big enough, to persuade the men in the village to listen to him. He could not stand guard all day and all night. He could not hide the sheep so they would not be found.

All that he could do was take the very best care of them possible, and hope that all would be well. Perhaps he could find a better grazing place, perhaps they should be nearer the stream where they could drink water without going far to look for it.

They were grazing peacefully, so he walked off a little way to see where the grass seemed greener. At the foot of the hill, and over a small rise, was a corner of the field where the stream spread out and became shallow. Unfortunately, a thicket of thornbush surrounded the area. Once, his father had told him, the thornbush had grown so thickly that much of the land could not be used. Since then it had been cut down and destroyed until only patches of it remained on the farm.

His grandfather, who had traveled a great deal, knew of places where cantuffa and other thornbushes grew so thickly that one could not go through it without hacking a path in advance. He had told Teffera about the old days when the emperor had traveled throughout the country with his court, and the proclamation he had put forth each time he began his trips.

"Cut down the cantuffa in the four quarters of the world, for I know not where I am going."

If Teffera were the emperor, he could order that the thornbush be cut down so he could herd the sheep into the pasture near the stream where they might be healthier. He was not the emperor, of course, but only a boy. He walked back to the sheep and tried to think of something else he could do.

For the next few days everyone was very busy getting his father ready to make his journey. All of his clothes were washed and made shining white, extra food was cooked for him to take. Teffera's mother would go with him to see the hospital with her own eyes and then come home again with Bekele.

Retta came over often to see Teffera, and every day he had more stories to tell about the ferangi and the terrible things they were doing in the next village. It was well known that Retta's father was a great gossip, who spent more time in the tej houses talking than he did caring for his farm.

"They cut the wool from the sheep's backs, so that they will freeze to death when the cold weather comes," he reported. "Perhaps they do it to shame us, because without their wool the sheep are very skinny and their bones stick out. In their country, they say, the sheep are all fat, whether they have wool or not."

One day he had different news.

"There is going to be a school in our village," he said. "Next year they will build a big building, and every one must give money to pay for teachers. All of us will be made to go, and we will have to learn to be like the ferangis."

"That is foolish," said Teffera. "How can I go to school? I must stay here and care for the sheep."

"By next year the sheep will all be dead," said Retta, "if the ferangis have their way."

Teffera did not believe everything Retta said, but he was more determined than ever to keep his sheep safe. When his father came home from the hospital, he would like to be able to show him that he had done a good job.

One day, on the slope of the hillside, a wonderful idea came to him. Others had cut the thornbush, why couldn't he? If he made a passageway through the thicket, he could herd the sheep through it, and use the bush he had cut to block up the opening. Then the sheep would be hidden, and if the ferangis came they would not be able to find them.

He began immediately, and found it very difficult work. The thorns were sharp and no matter how careful he was, he could not keep from getting stuck. After an hour his hands and arms were sore, and he was so tired that he had to quit.

Even so, he had made a good beginning. And no matter how hard the task, it would be worthwhile if it kept the sheep safe.

At last the day came when Paulos was to leave, and Teffera suddenly realized what it would mean to have him gone. Never had the family been without a father, and how would they fare without him? It made it worse to think that no one could be sure when he would be back, for no one knew what would happen in the hospital, or how long it would take them to make his eyes well.

Teffera and his parents would ride to the next village on horseback, and then his father and mother would take a bus to Uncle Bekele's home, while Teffera came home alone. Uncle Bekele had offered to meet them in the village so they would not have to take a bus, but Paulos's pride was very strong, perhaps more so because of his blindness. This much of the trip he and his wife could make alone. After that, Bekele would drive them to Addis Ababa, where neither of them had ever been.

Teffera's mother would worry because she could not stay at the hospital with her husband, but there were too many things at the farm demanding her attention. She would have to trust him, this man who was dearer than her own life, to the hands of people she did not know, strangers of an alien way. But at least she would be able to see them and the hospital and that would comfort her in the lonely days ahead.

At the last moment, before his parents boarded the bus, both of them held Teffera close and kissed him many times. Paulos's arms felt very strong and secure and Teffera knew how much he depended on that strength.

37

"The farm is yours while I am away," his father said. "God will be with you."

Teffera stood by the dusty road and watched the bus drive slowly out of sight; his eyes misted and a big lump arose in his throat that he could not swallow. He was happy that their whole village had gathered to say good-bye to his father, and that the priest had blessed him before he left. Now it was all in God's hands.

That afternoon he cut a great deal of thornbush, his sorrow seeming to give him new strength and courage. By the next day he would be ready to drive the sheep into their refuge, if it seemed necessary.

In the early evening Retta came to the house in great excitement. The servant girl had given Teffera his food, but he had not been able to eat much. The house and the courtyard seemed empty and forlorn with both of his parents gone, and he had never felt so alone in his life.

Retta's eyes were big with the story he had to tell. Eagerly he pulled Teffera out of the house, and whispered in his ear.

"There is a ferangi in the village," he said. "He came in a car this afternoon and made a camp for himself in the hill above the town. I suppose he thinks that he is hidden, but I have been watching him. Come on and I'll show you."

Teffera found a boy to watch the sheep, so he could go. This was too exciting to miss!

They went through the village and then started climbing the hill, going far to the left of where Retta said the ferangi was camped.

"We'll make a big circle and come out in the trees above him, so we can look down and see what he is doing. I'll show you where I hid this afternoon."

The ferangi's camp was set up in a clump of trees on the side of the hill near a small stream of water. There was a tent made of dark green cloth; in front of it the ferangi knelt before a fire burning in a metal container.

"Is he praying to a devil?" Teffera asked in a whisper.

"No, he's cooking something. He carries fire in the metal box and uses it to cook his food."

They were very quiet while they watched to see what he would do next. The ferangi's back was turned, but somehow it looked familiar to Teffera. He touched Retta's arm.

"He looks like Mr. Sam Jones," he said softly. "The ferangi I saw in my uncle's house."

"How can you tell?" asked Retta scornfully. "All ferangis look alike."

Teffera had heard that that was so, but when he had been in the hospital he had learned to tell one ferangi from another. There had been a tall slim one with red hair, and another short fat one with dark hair. Even those who were almost the same had some differences if you looked closely enough. In spite of the fact that they all had pink faces, and most of them had loud harsh voices, it was possible to tell one from another.

The ferangi turned from the fire and he had a glimpse of his face.

"It *is* Mr. Sam Jones," he said. "I am sure of it."

"Shhh! He'll hear you. Watch what he's doing now!"

The man went into the tent and came out, holding a small box in his hand. He did something to it, and suddenly music could be heard all around them.

"What is that?" Retta asked, in fear.

Teffera felt very wise.

"It is called a radio," he said. "My uncle has one. It is a box filled with voices and music, and when one turns a knob, they come out."

"It is magic," declared Retta. "I am afraid he is a very bad man. Let's go now, so I can tell my father about this."

As silently as they had come, the boys crept back down the hill, not daring to speak until they were in the village.

"What did I tell you?" Retta asked then. "I said that as soon as your father went, the ferangis would come. Now he will kill the sheep, and we will all starve to death."

5

THE RETURN

OF THE

FERANGI

Very early the next morning Teffera was out on the hillside, cutting thornbush and finishing his big project. If he worked as fast as he could, he might be just in time. Once the sheep were safely behind the barricade of thornbush, let Mr. Jones try to find them.

By now his hands were hardened to his task, and he was more skilled at dodging the thorns. His muscles, that had become soft and weak while he was in the hospital, were stronger than they had ever been.

At mid-morning he paused to look at what he had done. A gap had been cut in the thornbush, wide enough for two or three sheep to get through. Other thornbush had been cut down and piled high to complete a barricade that would fence them in and keep them from sight. All that remained was to herd them through the opening and close it behind them.

It had been a hard job, but his father would be proud of him when he saw what had been done. Teffera sat down on the hill-side in the midst of the herd that had been entrusted to his care, and felt very proud of himself.

Retta's voice interrupted his thoughts. "Teffera!" he said, "Let's go spy on the ferangi again! Let's see what he's doing this morning."

"Isn't he down in the village?"

"I didn't see a glimpse of him. My father thinks I am lying, that I made it all up, that there is no ferangi on the hill."

Teffera thought for a minute. His grandfather had said that in battle, it is very important to know what the enemy is doing, and so perhaps he ought to go with Retta.

But, on the other hand, it was not right for him to leave his sheep again. They were in his care in the daytime and his grand-father had also told him that a brave soldier does not desert his post.

"Why don't you go?" he suggested. "I must stay with my sheep, but I would like to know what the ferangi is doing."

Retta looked up in the sky and scuffed one of his bare brown toes in the ground.

"Perhaps it is not safe," he said. "I would feel better if you were with me."

Teffera laughed. "Are you afraid of him?" he asked. "Do you think he can harm you if he cannot see you? Are you not clever enough to creep up on him, as we did last night, so that he will not even know you are there?"

Retta did not like to be called a coward, or unskillful.

"All right, then, I will go! I will show you and the whole village that I am brave. You may stay here, if you like, I will go by myself."

It seemed very quiet and dull after Retta was gone and Teffera found himself thinking about his father again. By now he must be in the hospital, lying in one of the strange white beds and having needles stuck in him. He wondered how long it took to make eyes well? As long as it took to heal broken bones and cuts, or longer? If he missed him this much now, how would he feel as the days and weeks went by?

His uncle Bekele had said that it took many hours to go to Addis Ababa, even in a car, and it would take as many more for them to come home again. Until then, Teffera must get along by himself as best he could, and try to think what his father would want him to do.

It was a long time before Retta came back, hot, perspiring, and out of breath. He flung himself full length on the grass and let out a gasp of exhaustion.

"I ran all the way here," he said. "The ferangi is gone! His car is not there, and his tent is not there, and he left almost no sign that he camped overnight. If I were not such a good tracker, I would think that you and I were crazy."

Proudly he told of how he had gone over the place where they had seen the stranger the night before, and had found the holes made by tent stakes, and flattened grass where the man had slept.

"Except for that," he said, "there is nothing. This Mr. Sam Jones, if that is who it is, is very clever. He did not want anyone to know that he was there, or to find out where he has gone."

"Perhaps he went to another place nearby," said Teffera, "where he could hide himself better."

"No, I thought of that. That is what took me so long. I walked all through the hills, very quietly, making no more noise than a shadow. He is not anywhere. Besides," he admitted, "the people in the village saw his car drive through very early this morning. If I had asked before I started, I could have saved myself all the trouble."

"Which way did he go?"

"To Sheleko, where the other ferangi are. He is going to join them, I think, and help them kill the sheep."

For the first time since his father had left, Teffera felt that he could relax. As long as the ferangi stayed in the other village, he had nothing to worry about.

If they should come here, he could put his sheep behind the barricade, but until that happened they were all right where they were.

"Why do the men in Sheleko let them kill their sheep?" he asked. "When my father comes back, he will not let them."

"Oh, perhaps they are stupid or afraid," said Retta casually. "Everyone knows that their village is not as good as ours. If the ferangis come here, I will get one of my father's guns and drive them away."

Teffera could not remember Retta being so brave until the ferangi had actually gone, but he did not say anything about it. Picking up his long whip, he snapped it in the air until it sounded as loud and sharp as the sound of a bullet.

"Perhaps I can frighten them away with this," he said sarcastically.

"You may joke about the ferangi, but they are not sheep to be trained by your whip and your whistle. They are dangerous, evil men, and we must be on guard against them."

The days that followed passed very slowly, and Teffera had much time to consider what Retta had said. If danger should come, he would have to defend his village and the farm, and it would take all of his wit and courage.

Suddenly the dullness that had settled on his life was broken. The strange car that the ferangi had driven came to a halt in front of the courtyard, and Teffera's heart pounded with excitement. Retta had told him about it, and how it climbed rough trails as easily as a burro.

The front door opened, and to his amazement his mother stepped out. Close behind her was his uncle Bekele. Forgetting caution, he ran to greet them.

His mother covered his cheeks with kisses and wiped happy tears from her own face.

"Your father is well," she said. "He is very patient and very

44

brave, and the people at the hospital are good. I talked to the doctor myself, and he says they can cure your father's eyes, but they do not know how long it will take.

"They are good people, Teffera," she said. "I saw how kind they are, and how skilled. We must not worry about your father now. When he comes back to us again, his eyes will be as strong as an eagle's."

Even before Teffera had time to realize how happy he was, another man got out of the car. It was the ferangi, Mr. Sam Jones.

Ato Bekele placed his hand on the foreigner's arm affectionately and invited him inside the house, motioning to Teffera to follow.

Almost at once the two men began talking seriously.

"Things are pretty bad in Sheleko," Mr. Sam Jones said. "Our men tried to show them better ways of raising sheep, but they didn't make themselves clear. Now the whole village is up in arms, and the program is about to fall through."

Bekele nodded solemnly. "I know all about it," he said. "That is why I think this plan is better. We will go to the Tuesday Market, and I will introduce you. I will even ask my father to come to speak for you. Then people will know that they can trust you, and they will listen to what you say."

Mr. Sam Jones scratched his head. "Well, I don't know," he said, doubtfully. "After what I saw in Sheleko, I don't know that I'm very anxious to take someone's sheep and begin work. I'm not even sure it would be safe."

A broad smile spread over Ato Bekele's face. "That is all taken care of," he said. "I have talked this over with my brother, and you have permission to use his sheep. Everyone can come here and watch you, and see what happens. Then they will be glad to follow your advice about their own sheep. You wait and see—it will be very simple."

Teffera was so surprised and so frightened that he could not think for a minute, and then he knew what he must do. Very

45

slowly he began edging toward the door, trying to get outside before he was noticed.

It was easier than he had thought, because they were far too busy with their plans to pay any attention to him.

Quickly he went out of the courtyard and up to the hillside where his sheep were grazing. He dismissed the boy who had been taking his place so he could work alone. There was not time to put them all behind the barricade, and besides, it would not work. He could not hide all of the sheep and tell Mr. Jones they had died; his uncle would know he was lying.

Some of them, then, must be sacrificed. He went through the flock, selecting the best and strongest to drive behind the barricade. The others he left outside. It would be a tragedy to lose them, but at least a few of the finest would be saved for his father.

When it was all over, he returned to the house. Mr. Sam Jones and his uncle were still talking, making plans to go to the Tuesday Market. They would take the car, and invite as many men of the village as could be persuaded to go, so that they could hear Mr. Jones talk.

Not for the first time, Teffera wished that he were grown. He did not want to hear Mr. Jones talk, but it would be fun to go to the market and see all of the people and look at all of the things for sale or trade.

To his surprise, Mr. Jones seemed to notice him for the first time.

"Why don't you ride with me, Teffera?" he asked. "After all, you and I are already friends, and you can tell me more about the sheep on the way."

Teffera knew that he should refuse. It was not loyal to his father to have anything to do with this terrible plan. But in the absence of his father he must obey his uncle, and so he looked toward him.

48

Ato Bekele nodded. "That's a good idea," he said. "After all, Teffera, I won't be here all the time, and you'll have to work very closely with Mr. Jones."

This was something Teffera could not imagine, but he did not wish to say so. Before he could speak, he felt Mr. Jones's strong hand clasp his shoulder.

"You and I are going to be good friends, Teffera. I've got a boy about your age at home, and you'll keep me from missing him so much."

It was very hard for Teffera to go to sleep that night. His head was whirling with all of the things that had happened, and with feelings that he could not understand. All of his life he had heard of the terrible things done by the ferangis, and yet there was something he could not help liking about Mr. Sam Jones.

6

THE WORDS

OF THE

FERANGI

IT WAS not the first time Teffera had been to the Tuesday
Market, but the last time seemed long ago. With his father's
eyes getting worse, he had been needed to do more on the farm,
and the family had fewer sheep and less crops to trade than before.

This time they took very little. Teffera was sure his uncle
Bekele had brought gifts of things like kerosene and salt which
they would need, but part of the excitement of market would be
missing. There was nothing he loved more than to hear two
traders arguing about the merits of their products; each trying
to get the better of the other.

Just before they left, Mr. Sam Jones asked him if he wouldn't
like to take someone with him.

"Three of us can ride in the front seat, if two of us are boys,"
he said. "My youngster in America always has a friend he wants
to take along."

Teffera had rushed to invite Retta. If Mr. Sam Jones began to ask questions, a very unpleasant habit ferangis seemed to have, it would be easier to have Retta present to answer some of them.

"My boy is about your age," Mr. Sam Jones said, as they drove out of the village. "I wish he could be here with me, but he has to go to school."

Retta and Teffera nodded politely.

"I had a letter from him last week, and he wants me to send him more pictures of your country. He tells his class in school all of the things I write to him."

Teffera was not sure what all of this meant, but he was too busy looking out of the windows to worry much about it.

"Does your father raise sheep?" Mr. Sam Jones asked Retta.

"No, he raises teff."

"That's a cereal grain, isn't it? Does he get good crops?"

"Oh, yes, very good." Retta squirmed uncomfortably on the car seat.

All at once Mr. Sam Jones smiled broadly. "I keep forgetting something," he said. "Before I came here, I read books about Ethiopia, and talked to people who had been here. They told me lots of things, but I get so interested in what I'm doing that I forget. I'll see if I can explain something to you.

"I come from America, a big land thousands of miles away from here. America is a young country, compared to yours, and we do many things differently.

"If you visited America, even if you had read about it beforehand, there would be things that puzzled you and interested you. The only way you could understand, and get to know people, would be to talk and ask questions. In our country, we don't think it's impolite to ask questions. In yours, you do. So when I ask questions, it isn't because I'm being rude, but because I want to know more about you. If you want to know more about me, just ask, and I'll try to tell you."

Teffera could think of many things he wanted to know, but he did not think he would ask them. Retta was more bold.

"I have heard some ferangis went to Sheleko, and did very strange things," he said, his eyes round and innocent as if he knew no more than he was saying. "I heard that they cut the wool from sheep so they would be cold, and killed some of them, and stuck needles in some of them. Is this wicked story true?"

Mr. Sam Jones threw back his head and roared with laughter. "Retta, I'm glad you came with us! You know I'm going to talk to the farmers at the market, and I want you to listen to every word I say. Will you promise me that? Then you'll find out about the sheep in Sheleko."

The car made the final turn in the road and came upon the field that was used for the market. In the center grew a huge bamboula tree, and already crowds of people were gathered under its branches. Booths had been set up in the form of a square, and people with goats and sheep and chickens and cattle to trade were established in the midst of the crowd.

When the car stopped they could hear the beautiful, exciting noise of many people talking at once, through the sound of music. No fair was complete without groups of strolling musicians whose songs told of bravery in hunting and war, or of some form of generosity.

As the boys got out of the car, Mr. Sam Jones handed each of them a coin. "Here," he said. "Is a simuni each enough for some sugar cane?"

The boys agreed that it was, and thanked him, and then dashed off to see where the most excitement was brewing. Here were two women displaying fine cotton shemmas they had woven; next to them was a stall with donkeys loaded with sugar cane. Coffee was piled high, and a stack of sheepskins, the hair dirty and matted, was being offered for sale by a very old man.

The boys walked by every stall and listened to every conversation, then wandered over to look at the livestock. Most of the sheep, Teffera saw, were no better than his. Mr. Sam Jones and his uncle Bekele, with some of the men from the village, were also studying the livestock, and Mr. Sam Jones seemed to have quite a lot to say. From the way the men listened, they found his words interesting.

A stirring in the crowd behind them caught their attention, and Teffera saw that his grandfather, Kagnazmatch Abraham, had arrived. Quickly the other men of their party joined him, and word went through the crowd that something was about to happen.

Kagnazmatch Abraham signaled for everyone to come close, and when they were quiet, he spoke.

"Mr. Sam Jones is going to speak to you. He has come from the distant country of America, and I know you will listen carefully to what he has to say."

Mr. Sam Jones spoke for quite a long time. He told about coming from his own country because he was interested in Ethiopia and wanted to know more about it. He said that many years before other Americans had come to Ethiopia to study the crops and find grains which would grow well in America.

"You have crops that we do not have," he said, "and today grain from your country is growing in mine. Now I am here to see if I can help you with some of the things we know about sheep.

"It is always difficult to go into a different country and to speak a different language and make yourself clear to others. Most of you have heard what happened in Sheleko. Some of our men, who wanted to help, were trying to improve the breed of sheep. Perhaps they went too fast, or perhaps they did not explain what they were doing well enough. Terrible stories were told, and men became angry. We do not want that to happen.

"My friend Ato Bekele Abraham asked me to come here to talk with you and show you what we would like to do. He has said that we may work with the sheep of his brother, Ato Paulos

Abraham, and that all of you may come to see what we are doing.

"Then, if you like what you see, we will help all of you learn the things that we have to teach. Perhaps the things that we teach about sheep may flourish in your country, just as your grain is flourishing in mine."

Teffera had to admit to himself that it sounded very good and he wanted to believe what Mr. Sam Jones was saying. He could not help wondering, though, if the beautiful flower of the words concealed, somewhere, a very sharp thorn.

7

THE DAY
OF THE
MARREFIA BET

"THE first thing we must do," Ato Bekele said, "is to build a marrefia bet for Mr. Jones. He will be with us for some time, and it will be more comfortable for him than his tent." There was one thing that could be said for Uncle Bekele, and that was that things moved very swiftly when he was around. If he had been a general in the army, he could not have organized people better.

Before anyone had time to think and argue about why a guest house should not be built, or why it should be placed in one spot and not another, Ato Bekele had a group of men clearing a spot not far from the pasture where the sheep were kept.

Some began digging the circular ditch where the walls would be. Mr. Sam Jones worked with them. It was clear that his muscles were as clever as his tongue, because he tossed the red earth from the trench as rapidly as he had talked the day before.

Other men felled tall slim eucalyptus trees, and cut the

branches from them. Little boys stood around watching, and as a particularly good and leafy branch was severed, they grabbed it eagerly. Teffera, busy with the men, looked at the children rather wistfully as they rode their tree horses, switching the leafy tails boldly, and remembered when he, too, had been but a small boy. Then his hair had been cut with a tuft in the front, and he had had no deeper care than to prove his own tree horse the bravest and swiftest of all.

The eucalyptus poles were set deep in the trench at regular intervals, and chopped grass was added to the dirt as it was replaced. Enough water was put in it to make the mixture, called chicka, pliable and then it was pounded in place where it would dry almost as hard as a rock.

Once the poles were all in place, they were reinforced with smaller split branches woven through them, and the work of plastering with chicka began. Teffera had helped with this before, and he knew that the chicka from their own particular earth and chopped grass would make strong substantial walls that would keep out the cold of winter and the rains of the wet season.

In quite a short time the poles could be laid for the roof, and the thatching, which men of this village did especially well, could be started.

Uncle Bekele called Teffera from his work. "Mr. Jones wants to look at the sheep," he said. "Will you take him?"

Now Teffera was struck with the daring of what he had done. Would his uncle remember how many sheep there were? Would someone realize how many were missing, and ask awkward questions? His feet seemed to freeze to the ground and he was not sure that he could make them move. Then he remembered that he came from a family of brave men, and forced himself to go forward.

As casually as he could, he pointed out the sheep still in the main pasture to Mr. Sam Jones, who studied them carefully. Watching him as he walked among the sheep, stopping now to rub his hand over the back of one, then to study the wool of another, Teffera saw that one thing the ferangi had said was true—he was a man who knew and understood sheep.

When the ferangi was finished, he turned to Teffera.

"They're in pretty bad shape, aren't they? I must say I'm rather surprised. From what your uncle said, I had no idea the situation was so drastic."

Perhaps something in Teffera's face gave him away. Perhaps his eyes, against his will, darted to the thornbush barricade behind which the good sheep were hidden. Mr. Jones looked very thoughtful and began walking across the pasture.

"Your uncle talked so much about what a good farmer your father is, I thought your sheep would be healthier than most."

This was an insult, but Teffera said nothing. He wanted to shout out the truth, that these were only the very worst of the flock, but he dared not.

Mr. Jones kept walking, this time directly toward the thornbush.

"I wish you would trust me, Teffera, and believe that I only want to help. After all, what harm can I do? Your uncle is here, and your grandfather is not too far to come if you need him. You can watch me every minute, and ask me questions about anything you don't understand."

There was no doubt about it. Mr. Sam Jones was walking directly toward the thornbush!

"This is pretty mean stuff, isn't it?" he asked, as they got near. "I've seen it used for a fence, and it certainly keeps livestock inside. I don't know any animals that would try to work their way through it." He stopped and looked Teffera straight in the eye.

How had he known? Was he a magician, as Retta had said? Could he see through the thick barrier of thornbush to the sheep inside, or worse yet, could he look through Teffera's eyes straight into the truth?

Instead of going further, Mr. Sam Jones sat down on the ground. "You know, Teffera," he said, "if I were a boy like you, and I thought someone planned to hurt my sheep, I think I'd try to stop him. If I were very clever, I might make a wall of thornbush and hide my best sheep behind it." He waited, as if he knew that Teffera would talk. When this did not happen, he spoke again. "Your father and your uncle talked on the way to the hospital. Your uncle explained what I was trying to do, and your father said that the sheep were getting worse and might all die. He decided that it might be worth it to try something different. Do you think that's true?"

Teffera remembered that his grandfather had introduced Mr. Sam Jones to the people at the fair, and that his uncle had agreed with everything they had said. His father had told him to take care of the sheep, but he had also told him to obey his uncle and his grandfather. If this was a trick, he was helpless and could do nothing about it.

"They're behind the thornbush," he said.

Mr. Sam Jones did not move. "And they're your best ones, aren't they? If I were in your place, I know they would be. All right, I'll make a bargain with you. We'll leave those sheep right where they are, and we'll tell everyone we put them there. If we left all of the sheep together and did the same things to all of them, we couldn't be completely sure that what we were doing worked. But if we keep part of them in one place, and you take care of them as you always do, and we keep the others outside and I take care of them, then we can compare the two groups. Does that seem like a good idea?"

Teffera tried to think if there was more to this than there seemed. "It sounds all right," he said.

"Well, think of it this way. Suppose you had a headache, and took medicine to cure it. When your headache went away, you couldn't be really sure whether it just went by itself, or whether the medicine cured it. Isn't that true?"

Teffera nodded. He had heard men argue about this sort of thing, whether the wogesha really cured them, or whether the will of God would have made them well without the wogesha.

"But if two people had the same kind of headache, and one of them took medicine and the other one didn't, you could tell whether the medicine worked or not. In America, we call that setting up test conditions. So, if it's all right with you, we'll set up test conditions for the sheep."

There was nothing Teffera could do but agree. In a way, the ferangi was being kind, because Uncle Bekele would have been very angry if he had learned what Teffera had done. This way, he would never know.

Mr. Sam Jones put out his hand. "In America, when we agree on something, we shake hands."

Teffera extended his own, and felt it squeezed and pumped up and down.

"So that's settled. Now let's get back to the others, and tomorrow we'll begin work." He paused and a smile pulled the corners of his lips up. "And I'm not magic, Teffera. I was out last night, checking up, and I saw what you had done."

8

A LETTER

FROM

ADDIS ABABA

Mr. JONES had called the men of the village together to look at the sheep and discuss them. "Let me ask you a question first," he said. "Is it better to have a few sheep, or many?"

The men looked at each other suspiciously. This was a trick question, one that would trap them into saying something unwise. At last an elder of the village spoke.

"Do not think we are children," he said. "We do not understand your question, because there can be only one answer to it. Therefore we wonder why you have asked it."

Mr. Sam Jones put his head back and laughed heartily. "You are right," he said. "It is a trick, because you would say one thing, and I would say another, but the answer would be the same. In Shekelo, some of the men who work with me killed some sheep and this made everyone angry. The farmers thought we were making the flock smaller, but we were really making it larger."

The men muttered something among themselves and their voices were angry. Mr. Jones raised his hand.

"Let me explain," he said. "You and I are different, but we have many things in common. We do not look alike or speak alike or even think alike, but we can laugh together. When I asked my question I was making a joke." He reached down and picked up a handful of pebbles. With his other hand he took two coins from his pocket. "Which is worth more?" he asked. "Two coins or many pebbles?"

Someone in the crowd laughed.

"That's right," said Mr. Jones. "Now look at the sheep. There are many of them, but they are more like pebbles than coins. Some of them have one thing wrong, some another. It would be better to have a few good sheep than to have many poor ones. The good ones will have better lambs, and when those lambs grow up their own lambs will be good. In a few years the small flock will become a large flock, but they will all be good sheep."

A tall slender man, who believed nothing that anyone said, laughed sharply. "But how do we know that you can do what you say? In Sheleko, the fleece was cut from the sheep so that they were too cold. How could that make them stronger?"

Mr. Jones bent and picked a few dry blades of grass that had gone to seed. He showed them the sharp seed pods. "When a sheep is in full fleece, these stick in the wool and work their way into the flesh. They make sores that may become infected. Insects work their way into the fleece and may make the sheep sick. If the wool is sheared during the season when there are insects and seed pods, this can't happen. Sheep grow their heavy fleece for the winter time, and it gradually falls out during the summer. When we shear them, we are just taking off the wool quickly instead of waiting for it to fall out."

"But if God wanted the sheep to lose their wool quickly, why did He not arrange it that way?"

Mr. Jones looked around him. "I do not see one man among

you who lets his hair grow long. If God does not mind men cutting their hair, why should He mind if men cut the wool from sheep?"

The villagers nodded. Perhaps there was something in what the ferangi said. At any rate, they knew about the sheep safely behind the barricade which would prove whether or not he was right.

"Anyone can pick up pebbles," Mr. Jones went on, "but one must work to get coins. To raise good sheep, one must work very hard to keep them healthy. Look at this one for a moment."

He pointed to a ewe that was walking apart from the rest of the flock, and limping. Quickly he laid her carefully on her side and showed them a swollen hoof.

He motioned them to come near so that they could watch him and took a pair of tweezers and a sharp knife from his pocket. From a large wooden box he removed a pair of shears. Working rapidly, he cut the wool from around the hoof and then pulled a small stone from between the toes of the sheep.

"There doesn't seem to be much infection here, so the hoof will heal quickly on this dry ground. If it had been let go, the sheep would probably have become crippled. You see, none of the things I want to do is magic, but is just common sense."

All morning he worked, asking the men to help him when they wished. For the first time in his life Teffera saw a sheep shorn of its ragged, uneven wool, and left thin and almost naked. He saw the same sheep sprayed with a medicine to kill insects. It made him think of all of the strange things that had happened to him in the hospital.

"I have salt troughs to put in the field," Mr. Jones said. "We'll put some medicine in with the salt, so they'll all get a certain amount every day."

He mixed a fine white powder with the granulated salt as he filled the troughs, and Teffera knew that this was what he had mentioned when they had met. In spite of all he had planned,

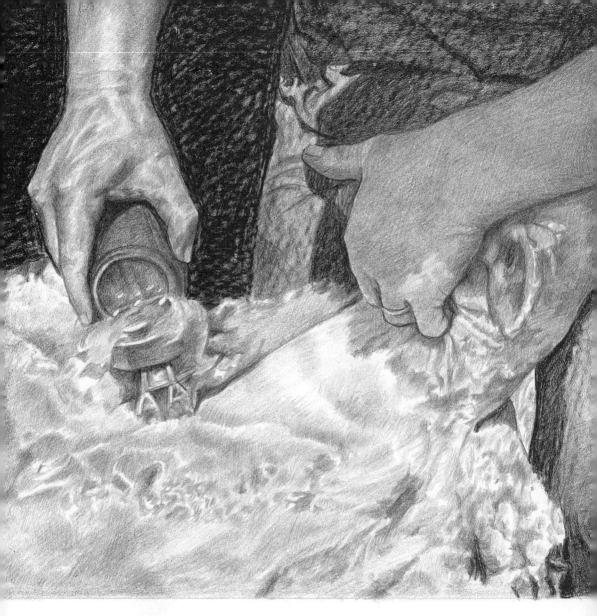

his sheep were going to have the white powder of the ferangis
after all! But was it dangerous and evil? He could not tell. Nothing that Mr. Sam Jones had done so far seemed bad, but when
men work mischief they hide it from the eyes of others. Sometimes a smiling face conceals a heart black with hatred.

66

When it was time to go to the house to eat, Teffera was so full of new ideas he felt as if his head would burst. It was plain that Mr. Sam Jones knew a great deal about sheep, but was his wisdom good for these particular sheep? Perhaps these things were good for the sheep of ferangis, but not for others—perhaps they were not good for any sheep, but only part of a wicked and secret plan. How could he tell?

The men in the village were now divided. Some of them, the ones who liked change and excitement, thought that everything they had seen was wonderful. Others were still doubtful and suspicious. Teffera could listen to them as they talked and find out what they thought, but he needed more. If only he could talk to his father, and explain everything he had seen and heard, and see what his opinion was. If only he knew more about America, and about what Mr. Sam Jones had done in other places in Ethiopia, and what had happened there. But how could that be? He could not travel to America, or even to the places Mr. Jones had been. Suddenly he felt as if the world around him was covered with a thick mist, through which he could see only the things nearby that he had known since he was a child.

Teffera's mother met them at the door with a happy smile on her face. She held out her hand and showed them a letter. "This came today from Paulos," she said. "He has written us a letter from Addis Ababa. This afternoon the scribe will come to the house and read it to us."

"Would you like me to read it to you?" asked Mr. Jones. "I may not be able to do as well as the scribe, but I'll do my best."

She gave it to him happily. It was clear that she trusted him and liked him.

Mr. Jones opened the envelope and took out the folded paper.

"To my beloved family," he read. "I give great thanks to God that all is well with me and I trust that you are prospering under His care.

"This is a very strange place, and I am lonely for my home, but the people here are good. They have done many things to my eyes, and now there are bandages over them so that I cannot see at all.

"Fortunately, there is a scribe here at the hospital just as there is in our village, so I can write to you and tell you all that is happening. I hope you will send me a letter and let me know how things are with you.

"In many ways Bekele is right in what he says of the ferangi. I have heard many tales of wonders they have done in curing the sick, and I believe most of them are true. Not everything I hear, however, is good.

"I am tired and must rest now. May God have you in His keeping.

Paulos Abraham"

The eyes of Teffera's mother were misted with tears. "Thank you very much," she said. "It makes it seem that he is not away from us, but close by."

"That's the way I feel when I get a letter from home," Mr. Jones said. "It makes me miss my family more, and feel closer to them at the same time."

"Then you have scribes in your villages, just as we do in ours?" Teffera's mother said.

Mr. Jones shook his head. "No, almost everyone in our country knows how to write. There is a school in every town, and our children go to school from the time they are six until they are grown. I had a long letter from my son, who is about Teffera's age, just last week. Here's his picture, if you'd like to see it."

He pulled a square of cardboard from his pocket, and Teffera and his mother looked at it. The boy they saw was as tall and slim as Teffera, but his hair and face were pale.

"It would be good if Teffera could write," said his mother. "Perhaps next year he will go to school and learn."

"Learning to write is difficult; but a bright youngster like Teffera won't have much trouble. Your schools are doing a wonderful job."

Something stirred inside of Teffera. If he went to school and learned to write, could he not also read what others had written?

69

By reading, could he not learn what was now hidden from him? He felt as he had when his grandfather had talked of hunting and war and he had shared the excitement of seeking for wild beasts in the jungle. Like the quarry of the hunter, something very precious was almost before his eyes, almost where he could reach out and touch it.

After lunch, Mr. Jones took him to one side. "I just had an idea, Teffera. If you'd like to send a letter to your father, I'll write it for you. You can tell me what you want to say, and I'll put it on paper. Would you like that?"

This was a gift that Teffera could not refuse. It would not be quite the same as talking to his father face to face, but it would be like reaching out a hand toward him. He could put into words the things he had thought about all morning, and send his thoughts and questions to his father. Such a message could go where he could not go, through the miles of the outside world and straight to his father's mind.

9

THE FEAST

OF THE

NEW YEAR

In the evening, Teffera and his mother told Mr. Sam Jones all that they wanted to say to Paulos, and he put it in a letter.

Teffera had watched the village scribe write letters but it was such a strange process he had never paid much attention to how it was done. Now, watching Mr. Sam Jones, who was not a scribe, make the mysterious marks on paper, it seemed very different. He tried to think why this was so.

A scribe was a wise man who knew what his neighbors did not—just as the priests had knowledge of God that the ordinary man did not, so did the scribe have strange arts of his own. Teffera would no more have wondered how it was done than he would have wondered how a priest knew the will of God, or how a weaver knew how to make a beautiful pattern in the cloth on his loom.

Mr. Sam Jones acted as if writing itself were something to take for granted, but he did not pretend that it was easy. "Your language is much older than mine, and much more complicated," he said. "We only have to learn twenty-six different letters, but you must learn more than 250."

When it was finished, they all breathed sighs of relief. It was a difficult task to take the thoughts from your mind and shape them into words to put on paper.

"Shall I sign both your names?" asked Mr. Sam Jones, and Teffera nodded happily. He held his hand very still while the ferangi covered the ball of his thumb with ink, then pressed it on the paper to make a print. His eyes widened as the pen made letters around the thumbprint, letters that spelled his own name —Teffera.

He was eager for his father to see it, and yet he wished that he could keep it for himself. It was almost as if Mr. Sam Jones could read his mind. "Would you like a copy of your own?" he asked, and when Teffera nodded again, he repeated the process on a clean sheet of paper.

Teffera almost stuttered his thanks. He had had his name written before, but never by a ferangi, and especially by an Americour. His eyes drank in the strange marks that were beautiful like the twigs of an acacia tree against the sky, or the tracks made by the feet of birds in wet sand.

When his father saw these marks at the bottom of his letter, it would be almost as if he saw his own son. Wherever those marks went, they stood for him—Teffera. He would take good care of his name and keep it with him always.

Mr. Sam Jones looked at him and smiled. "Now there's something important for us to talk about. You remember how angry the villagers were in Sheleko when the Americans killed some of the sheep?"

Teffera nodded.

"Well, we've got the same problem here. Most of your sheep are going to be all right, I think, but we can improve the herd by getting rid of some of the worst ones. I don't want to go at it the wrong way, though, so I thought I'd ask you about it first."

Teffera's mother, who had been listening, broke in. "It will soon be the day of the New Year," she said, "and we always kill sheep for our feast. If you kill the poorer ones, though, we would not like to offer them to our guests."

Mr. Sam Jones thought for a minute. "Well, I think we could lick that. How long is it till New Year's Day?"

"Only a few days. This month is nearly ended and the first day of Maskaram is New Year's."

"Then we won't have time. I wanted to cull the sheep and fatten up the ones to be killed, but that wouldn't work. We'll have to think of something else."

"We must not shame our home," Teffera's mother said. "We must kill our best sheep for the New Year."

Mr. Sam Jones smiled at her. "Well, I won't quarrel with you about that. We don't have to cull the herd right now, anyway. Mascal is more important than New Year's, and they should be just right by then. In the meantime, I'd like to help with the feast for New Year's. I have to go back to town for some things, and if it's all right I'll bring something back with me."

For three days before the Feast of the New Year Mr. Sam Jones was gone, and Teffera was left to care for the whole flock. His own, behind the barricade of thornbush, seemed as well as ever, so far as he could see, but those of Mr. Sam Jones began to seem different. The shorn ones showed a little fat over their ribs and they were eating more heavily than before. Even so, they were not as strong and healthy as the ones he had selected as the best of the lot.

Every day, while he watched the sheep, he took the paper with his name on it and studied it. He would have liked to send it to his father as a gesture of love, and perhaps he would when it was time for another letter.

On the day before the feast Mr. Sam Jones arrived from the town with boxes in his car. Teffera helped him carry them into his guest house and Mr. Sam Jones explained what each contained.

"This is more spray, in case some of your neighbors want to try our methods, and this is more salt and medicine. Here are some shears, so I can teach others how to shear the sheep. And here is what I brought for the feast."

He showed the box full of round shiny tin cans, such as Teffera had seen at his uncle's home in town. At that time, when he had been so homesick, the ferangi food had not tasted good to him, but now he began to remember it with pleasure.

"Oh, yes, Teffera, I brought you something. Your mother said you might be going to school next year, so I brought you some tablets and pencils."

Teffera thanked him and then waited eagerly to be excused so he could run and show his mother the gift. Dozens of ideas were dancing through his mind. Having pencils and tablets of his own was like owning a straight and beautiful gun, because these were weapons to use in the struggle he felt would soon be his.

His mother looked at the gifts with his same excitement and helped him put them carefully away in one of the boxes where their most valuable possessions were stored.

"I have always known that you would be a great man," she said tenderly, "and the ferangi has seen it, too."

On the day of the feast the whole village began to gather and Retta came with a group of men that included his father. Teffera suddenly realized that he had not seen Retta for several days, and had not even missed him because so many things had been happening.

"How many of your sheep has the ferangi killed?" Retta whispered, when he had taken him to one side.

Teffera felt angry for no reason he could name.

"He has killed none of our sheep. He has given them medicine and helped them, but he has not hurt any of them."

74

"Wait and see," said Retta. "He will kill them. He will wait until you are no longer suspicious, and then he will do it."

"No, I do not believe that that is so. Mr. Sam Jones has told us about the world outside of Ethiopia, and why he has come here. I believe that he is our friend."

Retta laughed boisterously. "Well, do not worry, Teffera. Our teff is very good this year, and when there are no more sheep we will share our grain with you. Now let us go and listen to the men tell stories."

A group was gathered around a very old man who was known

throughout the countryside for his skill as a warrior. In his youth he had killed many lions, and now he was retelling each hunt in detail, just as it had happened so many years ago.

When he had finished a younger man told of the great battles fought by the soldiers of Ethiopia, and how the whole world had marveled at their courage and their endurance under great hardships. "In other parts of the world men fought, but they dug holes in the ground which they called trenches. They hid in these holes so their enemies could not see them. How could men so frightened be brave enough to fight?"

This was a question no one could answer. Every Ethiopian boy was taught from birth that courage and strength and endurance were expected of him, but in other countries this was obviously not the case.

Great tables had been set up for the feast and there was much tella to drink, and much injerra and many kinds of wett to eat. When everyone was full the wonderful old songs were sung, and Retta's father was called upon to tell their favorite stories. Teffera and Retta and their friends listened eagerly, knowing almost every word exactly as it would be said, and enjoying it more because of that.

"The Tale of the Golden Earth," someone cried out from the crowd. Retta's father smiled and began his story.

"Once, many years ago, honorable men from a far country came to visit Ethiopia. His Imperial Majesty, our Emperor, received them graciously and entertained them well. He gave them guides so they could see all of the wonders of our land, and had many big feasts in their honor.

"When it was time for them to return to their home, he sent guides with them as far as the frontier. Before the guests departed, the guides asked them to remove their shoes, and very tenderly they helped to take them from their feet.

"Then the guides brushed and washed the shoes and returned them, and the foreigners were puzzled.

76

" 'Why have you done this?' they asked.

"The guides stood tall and spoke clearly.

" 'His Imperial Majesty, the Emperor, has been pleased to have you as his guests and to show you every courtesy at his command. He has shown you the many wonders of our land, and he has given you gifts to take home with you.

" 'However, as you walked upon the beautiful soil of Ethiopia, some small grains of it has gotten into your shoes. So precious to us is each small part of our beloved country that we have cleaned your shoes, so that not even a grain of it will leave our borders.' "

Everyone smiled and applauded because this was one of the stories liked best.

Retta's father smiled lazily. "Perhaps Mr. Sam Jones, who is now our guest from a strange country, would like to tell us a story?"

The ferangi got to his feet and moved toward the center of the crowd. "I don't think I'm as good at telling stories as you, but I'll read you one that someone wrote. Will that be all right?"

They nodded and smiled, and he took a paper from his pocket and began.

"A long, long time ago, a queen ruled in Ethiopia. Her name was Makeda, and she was known everywhere for her beauty and wisdom. Stories about her were told where ever men traveled, and stories about the rest of the world were told at her court.

"One thing that she heard interested her very much. In another country, far away, ruled a king named Solomon who was called the wisest man in the world. Queen Makeda thought about him more and more, because wisdom was highly prized in Ethiopia, and she knew that she must see him or she could never be happy.

"She sent word throughout her kingdom to bring gifts worthy of the mighty King Solomon, and she formed a great caravan to travel to the strange court.

"When she arrived King Solomon received her graciously and

77

everything happened as she had thought. His wisdom was like a bright light shining in the darkness to her, and her beauty was like a flower in a barren desert to him.

"The two fell in love, and Makeda bore Solomon's son, whom she called Menelik. The day came when she knew she must return to her own kingdom, but she promised that when the boy was grown she would send him to his father's court to be taught the arts of kingmanship.

"The years passed and the boy grew tall and strong and handsome. One day his mother sent him to his father, as she had promised. In the court of King Solomon he was treated with great honor and taught the wisdom of ruling. When he was ready to be a king, Solomon called him into his presence to give him his blessing.

"'Just as you are my greatest living treasure,' he said, 'so I will give you the greatest treasure in my kingdom to take back with you so that your country may belong to God forever.'

"Then the great King Solomon gave Menelik the stone tablets on which Moses had written the Ten Commandments given by God, and commanded him to take them back to Ethiopia as a gift to his people.

"So Menelik returned to the land of his mother, and the stone tablets were placed in a sanctuary where they are still kept today."

There was a long silence when he had finished, because this was a story each of them had heard from childhood. Their applause was loud.

Mr. Jones smiled at them. "This story is not told as well as you could tell it, and it is not exactly as I have heard it told. You saw that I read it from a paper, and the paper was sent to me by my son. Because I am in Ethiopia, he reads everything he can find about your country, and he liked this story so well he wrote it in his own words and sent it to me. He will be very proud to know that you liked it so much.

"Now I'd like to tell you something else. There are many different kinds of people in the world, and since we look and speak differently from each other it is hard for us to learn to be friends.

"When your Queen Makeda made her journey to visit Solomon, she must have met many hardships and often wondered if she were doing the right thing. His court and his people were strange to her, with different ways of talking and doing things, and sometimes she must have been frightened to be so far away from all that she knew and loved.

"She went to him with eagerness to share his wisdom, and from her daring great treasures came to her country. It seems to me that it's the same way with us—if we trust each other and share what we know, both of our countries will be richer and better for it."

Teffera saw that Retta was as moved by the ferangi's words as the others, and it made him feel very proud. After all, was not this ferangi the guest of his family, and therefore sent to them in peace by God?

"I will show you what the ferangi gave me," he whispered. Carefully he took the piece of paper from where he kept it hidden and unfolded it and showed it to Retta. "That is my name," he said. "Mr. Sam Jones wrote it for me to keep."

Now, at last, he had accepted the stranger and would try to doubt him no more. He could not suppress the thrill of triumph that went through him when Retta turned and walked away, too impressed by his possession to talk.

10

~~~~~~

THE SECRET

OF THE

NIGHT

V ERY early the morning after the feast Teffera checked on
his own sheep, then joined Mr. Sam Jones.

"Would you like me to help you?" he asked. "My sheep are
all right, and I can stay with you as long as I go to look at them
once in a while."

Mr. Sam Jones looked at him as if he hoped that Teffera's
doubts of him were gone.

"Why, yes. Thanks a lot, Teffera. As a matter of fact, I've been
thinking things over and I decided it would be better if I asked
several of the boys to help. They can be spared from the farms
better than their fathers, and if they see just what I'm doing
they'll be able to explain it to their parents better than I can.
Maybe I ought to go around the village today and talk to them,
if you'll just keep an eye on the sheep for me."

Somehow this did not please Teffera. He knew that the ferangi
said he had come to help the whole village, but he liked the

feeling that he was truly interested only in his own family. And how much more important he would feel if only he, Teffera, could explain to the others just what the ferangi was teaching!

He tried to put the thought down. If you trusted someone, as he was trying to trust Mr. Sam Jones, you trusted him all of the way and did not question what you did not understand.

"You see, I've only shorn a few of the sheep, because I want everyone to see that it helps them instead of hurting. I ought to finish the job and then get them all sprayed, because pests will spread from the infected ones to the others, but I've been trying to go slow. Why don't I go now and see how many helpers I can round up, and you stay here in charge until I come back?"

Teffera nodded, and Mr. Jones left, his hat pushed back from his eyes and whistling a foreign tune.

As soon as he was gone, Teffera began examining the sheep, and everything that Mr. Sam Jones had done, in great detail. It was not dignified to show too much curiosity in front of others, but now he could find the answers to things that had puzzled him.

He ran his hands through the rough matted fleece of the unshorn sheep and saw that there were, indeed, sharp seed pods and dirt and insects buried in it. Then he observed the naked ones that had had their coats removed and saw that they seemed cleaner and even fatter than a few days before.

He looked at the salt troughs and noted that the sheep were eating the salt, so they must like it. The flock still looked poor, but there was a change from the time when Mr. Sam Jones had begun.

Leaving that flock, he made his way through the opening in the thornbush, pushing the cut branches carefully aside, and looked over his own sheep.

There was one among them that stood out—a young ram he had watched since birth because it was stronger and handsomer than any of the rest. This one would sire many fine lambs, and he was almost tempted to put it with the sheep of Mr. Sam

Jones, as a token of his friendship and trust. But not yet, he thought—not until he was absolutely sure that Retta was wrong, and that the ferangi came only to improve and not to destroy.

His mind more at rest, but still in a pleasant turmoil of new ideas, he went back through the barricade and sat down on the hillside among the sheep. Drifting off into a daydream of the time when he would own many gashas of land covered with huge flocks of big, healthy sheep, he was rudely interrupted.

"Teffera! Teffera! Wake up! I have something to show you!"

It was Retta, out of breath from running, and holding a white paper in his hand. He was smiling, but there was a gleam of triumph in his eyes. "See what I have? It is my own name, written on this paper. *Your* friend," and the words were somehow scornful, "gave it to me, and asked me to help him, and he is doing the same for every boy in the village who will help."

Teffera felt as if the very ground beneath him had given way. The pledge of Mr. Sam Jones's special friendship for him had meant nothing—he had forgotten the one who had trusted him and helped him, and was treating everyone alike. Quickly he pulled himself together and smiled coolly.

"Oh, it means nothing," he said. "I did not think it was important. It is nothing for the ferangi to write a name. I only showed it to you because it was interesting."

Retta scowled at him. "You say that now, but you acted differently last night. Well, never mind. I shall keep my own name until next year when we have a school, and then I will learn to write it for myself. What does the ferangi want us to do to help? My father said it was all right, as long as I did not let his foreign magic overcome me."

Teffera shrugged and turned away. "He will tell you. As for myself, I must go and take care of my own sheep. This is only," his mind searched for the word Mr. Sam Jones had used, "an experiment, you know. My part is to stay with my own sheep and see that they are all right."

In spite of his pride, it was hard to stay behind the barricade in the afternoon and hear the laughing voices of the other boys as they worked with Mr. Sam Jones. By working cleverly he was able to make a peephole in the barricade through which he could watch what they were doing, and he could hear almost everything they said.

Mr. Jones was explaining about culling the sheep. "See this one," he said. "The body is narrow, and the legs are so close together they almost seem to grow from one spot. That means it won't have good lambs. Feel through the fleece and see how thin its bones are. A good sheep is solid and blocky with heavy bones, and those are the ones we want to save."

"Will you kill this skinny one?" It was Retta's voice, and Teffera could hear the mischief behind the pleasantness with which he spoke.

"Eventually, yes. But we don't want to waste it. That's what I want you boys to help me with. We'll build a pen here in the pasture, and put all of the sheep that should be culled in it. We'll keep them there a few weeks and give them extra feed to fatten them up. Then when we butcher them they'll be much better to eat."

All afternoon Teffera listened and watched and thought and eventually he knew what he must do. Mr. Sam Jones had talked about the experiment which would prove to everyone that his aims were good, but Teffera would make an experiment of his own. He would keep it secret from the whole world, and when the time came he would know whether the ferangi was to be trusted, or whether his evil aims must be exposed to the village.

There was a certain tree growing along the brook from which he could make a dye. He searched until he found one with many fresh leaves and stripped handfuls of them to use. He hid them under a stone until the darkness would let him proceed with his plan.

At the evening meal he pretended that all was as it had been before, and he was sure that Mr. Sam Jones noticed nothing. While no one was looking he found a vessel and the materials he needed to make a fire and hid them under his bed.

Long after everyone in the house had gone to sleep he got cautiously to his feet and crept out through the open door into the dark and silent night.

There were two shepherds who watched the sheep by night, one with Mr. Jones's flock and one inside the barricade he had built. He saw that they were together, talking quietly as they stood guard against hyenas or any other marauder that might disturb the flocks.

They greeted him with surprise. "I could not sleep," he said. "I was thinking of my father. I did not wish to disturb those in the house with my wakefulness so I came out here."

He sat down with them and talked for a while to allay their suspicions. When they had forgotten how strange it was to see him at such an hour, he made his offer.

"Since I cannot sleep anyway, I will watch the sheep inside the barricade if you like. My eyes are so wide open and my mind so alert no hyenas can come near, I promise you."

The man inside the barricade was happy to agree. There was no danger in accepting the offer, because Teffera's bravery and dependability were well known; besides, he was the son of the man who owned all of the sheep.

As soon as the two men were together and not too near the barricade he began what he had come to do, selecting a place beyond the curve of the hill and near the creek. Gathering twigs and bits of broken wood, he built a small fire and placed the vessel containing the crushed leaves and water over it. He let it simmer for a long time because the darkness did not allow him to tell for sure when the dye was dark enough, and he did not want to make any mistakes.

When he thought that it must be ready he took it from the fire and set it to one side to cool. Then began his hardest task—

searching through the flock for the prize ram, the one he knew was finest of all.

Remembering what Mr. Sam Jones had said, he felt of each sheep in turn until his hands told him that he had found one broader and stockier than the rest. Guiding it gently, he led it near the fire where the light from its flames would let him see it better.

No, it was the wrong one. Again he began his search, bringing sheep after sheep near the fire until he had discovered the one for which he searched.

Working carefully, he tilted the vessel and let the warm dye run on to the fleece on the ram's chest, using his hands to work it well down so that it would reach the skin beneath. He could not be sure that he had succeeded as well as he had hoped, but even a small spot of color, discovered at the right time, would give him the answer he needed.

His job completed, he set the ram on its feet and emptied the rest of the vessel into the stream so the water would carry away the traces of what he had done.

Then he sat down among his sheep, alert for any danger to them, and satisfied with the trap he had set for any evil the ferangi might do.

11

THE LIGHT

IN THE

MARREFIA BET

TEFFERA was too tired the next day to help the others build the pen, even if he had wanted to. Besides, he was still full of resentment that each of them had his name written on a piece of paper by Mr. Sam Jones.

He was proud of his clever scheme which was now half completed, but he could not share that pride with anyone since it must be kept secret. The nearer he came to being a man, the more he knew that he must do something, be something, that would make him stand out among others. Perhaps this was it, but it was hard to wait quietly until the time came to share his cleverness.

Lying on the hillside and listening to the voices outside the barricade, he tried to think of what he might do now. He went over his conversation with Retta the day before, when he had discovered that he was not the only one with his name written on paper. What was it that Retta had said? That when school started, he would learn to write his own name. Well, was he not as wise as Retta? Had not God given him a good mind, just as He had given Retta a beautiful voice and a love of jokes?

He had studied the marks that made his name until he could see them with his eyes shut. Could he make the same marks, all by himself?

He found a bare piece of ground by the stream and a small stick. The first mark—what was it? He shut his eyes and saw it clearly. A straight up and down line with a shorter line across the top. Carefully he made it on the ground before him. Was it the same? He could not be sure.

Since talking with Retta he had not carried his paper with him, but had put it in the box with the tablets and pencils Mr. Sam Jones had given him. Very well, then. He would get the paper, and also one of the tablets and a pencil. Mr. Jones had shown him how to sharpen it and he would do that.

Casually he walked by the others, speaking to them pleasantly and noticing how much of the pen was finished. No one saw him take the things from the box, and for that he was glad. It was not possible that he could not succeed in making his name, but it would be as well to do it before he told anyone what he planned.

He tucked the pencil and tablet inside the top of his mantle and returned again to the hillside, not wanting to stop, this time, even for a minute.

Mr. Sam Jones called out to him. "See how well we're coming along, Teffera! By this afternoon it should be finished. Then we'll get the sheep in and start fattening them up."

"And I will help you," thought Teffera, "but not as you think." Aloud he said, "It is very good. Perhaps later I will help you. Now I am feeling very tired."

Inside the barricade once more, he put a good point on the pencil with a razor blade and laid the paper with his name on it beside a fresh sheet of paper in the tablet. Gripping the pencil tightly in his fingers, he made the first mark, bearing down hard.

Just as he completed it, the lead snapped and he saw that he had made a hole in the paper.

Perhaps one should not hold the pencil so tightly or press so much. Again he sharpened the pencil and took a fresh sheet of paper. He copied the marks, but when he was finished they did not look the same. Some of his lines were one length and some another, and they did not all curl in the right places. They did not go evenly across the paper, as did those of Mr. Sam Jones, but made a crooked path.

Over and over again he tried it, his fingers growing numb and his mind growing ever more tired. He had to remind himself many times of his grandfather stalking lions and of the great weariness he must have felt. A brave man, he knew, did not stop what he wanted to do because of difficulty, but continued until he was successful.

Once he had to stop and rest, and a vague worry began to tug at his mind. He tried to think what it could be. It was something to do with his scheme and with the ram, but he could not place it. What was there to worry about? He had done what he planned, and it had been successful, because he had checked this morning. Peering down through the fleece, he had seen the mark of the dye on its skin.

The rest of the dye was gone, washed away in the stream, and the cleansed vessel had been returned to where it was kept. The shepherds of the night had not suspected what he was up to, and certainly Mr. Sam Jones knew nothing about it. What was it that warned him of a mistake, of the danger that he had forgotten something? Wearily he rubbed his eyes, but he could not think of the answer.

Again he picked up the pencil and tablet. This time his fingers were more accustomed to the task, and his practice had given him sureness. At last the marks took their proper places and shapes and he knew that he had succeeded! He had written his own name, Teffera, and though it seemed not as sure and even as

where Mr. Sam Jones had written it, it certainly looked almost the same.

A sense of pride went through him so sharply that he felt almost dizzy. Without any help, without being told by anyone, he had done what Retta could not do, what no other boy he knew could do! Like the wise men of his country and the ferangi, he had made marks on a paper that told a message to anyone who could read.

For a long time he could not take his eyes from the paper, but feasted them on it, savoring the skill with which each line had been drawn and each letter shaped. His father must know, his mother must know . . . the tumult of his thoughts was broken by the sound of his name.

"Teffera!" It was Mr. Sam Jones, standing near the barricade and calling him. Quickly he gathered all of his paper and the tablet and the pencil together and hid them under a large stone before he went to answer.

"What is it?" he asked, still almost breathless with what he had done, and with his hurrying.

"We finished the pen, and we're going to check through the flock now, and I thought you'd like to help us. I can give you some tips on how to judge sheep that ought to be useful for you."

Teffera followed him willingly, feeling as he walked that his feet barely touched the ground and that nothing could be so important as learning to write your name.

Mr. Sam Jones gathered the boys around him and walked over to the flock of sheep. "First we'll pull out the skinny ones—you know, like the one I showed you yesterday. Then, just for practice, we'll try judging their age. In this case it doesn't make much difference, but it's a handy thing to know."

He had each boy select a sheep he thought was inferior, and then discussed it with the group. When the worst ones had been separated from the flock and put in the pen, he had the boys join him there.

92

"The best way to judge a sheep's age is by 'mouthing' it," he said. "Sheep get their teeth at different times, as humans do, and you can judge pretty well by that. Then if someone wants to sell you a sheep and you want to be sure how old it is, you won't have to take his word. You can tell for yourself."

For an hour or more they practiced, and as Mr. Sam Jones had said, it was very simple once you understood it. At last even the youngest and slowest boy had mastered it, and Mr. Sam Jones was satisfied.

"Okay, boys," he said, "let's stop for a while. I think we've done a pretty good day's work. Tomorrow we'll shear all of these and spray them, so they'll be able to give their full attention to getting fat." His eyes lighted on Teffera, but just as he had said the word "shear," Teffera had realized what the vague worry was that had tugged at his mind. He wanted to turn on his heel and go back to the barricade, but Mr. Sam Jones was speaking to him. "Will you do us a favor, Teffera? Will you let us go in to your flock and look them over? With what the boys have learned this afternoon, they'll be able to see why you selected the ones you did."

Teffera stood rooted to the ground, his mouth refusing to open. His mind was working with the speed of a trapped animal trying to escape a snare. Suddenly he knew what he must do.

"You are welcome," he said, "but there is one thing first, if you do not mind? If you will stay here a minute, I would like to show you something."

Mr. Sam Jones smiled at him, as one trusted friend smiles at another. "Sure, Teffera."

Quickly the boy ran to the barricade and made his way through the opening, and uncovered the tablet that he had hidden. This secret must be sacrificed to save the other.

He went back to the group and stood in front of Mr. Sam Jones and handed him the tablet. "I wanted you to see what I did," he said, and then bowed his head and darted away. As he ran back toward the barricade he knew that they would think he was too shy to remain with them while they looked at his surprise, and that would give him time for what he must do.

Fortunately, the ram was on the edge of the flock and quickly located. Tugging at his wool, he led him to the stream and dipped handfuls of mud and rubbed them into the fleece. When he was finished the ram looked as if he had somehow gotten into a muddy place and wallowed through it. Teffera breathed a deep sigh of relief and went back to join the others.

The boys were clustered around, staring at the tablet, and Mr. Sam Jones had a smile on his face brighter than any Teffera had ever seen there.

"This is wonderful!" he said. "Teffera, you couldn't have done anything that would have made me prouder. Why, I feel like— well, I don't know, but like the first time my son took a step, I guess. Did you do this all by yourself?"

Teffera nodded.

"Then you're twice as bright as I thought you were, and I knew you were smart. You know, this gives me an idea. Would the rest of you boys like to learn to write? It will help you a lot when you start to school next year, and I'd like to teach you."

Retta, who did not look terribly pleased at the praise being heaped on Teffera, smiled mischievously.

"But how can you teach us to write when you are working with the sheep?"

"Oh, we'll have lessons at night. We can work in my marrefia bet."

"But it is dark at night, and the light of the fire is not enough for us to see."

"Now, Retta, you know better than that. Didn't I see you near my marrefia bet last night? You know I have a lantern there that makes the room almost as bright as day. Won't your parents let you come to my place for an hour or so every evening?"

The boys nodded. Their parents, though they might not trust

94

the ferangi, were eager for knowledge for themselves and for their families.

"Well, you ask them, and we'll see what we can do. Probably there won't be enough time for you to learn very much, but everything you do learn will put you that much ahead. I thought I came over here to work with sheep, but I can tell you that if even ten of you boys learned to write your names, like Teffera, I'd think that was the biggest job I ever did in my life."

Teffera nodded with the rest. Somehow he did not mind that all of the boys in the village would learn to do what he had done by himself, because he felt that he and Mr. Sam Jones were joined by a strong but invisible band. It was his own mind and his own hand that had formed the letters on the paper, but it was the pattern made by the ferangi that he had followed.

For the moment he was carried away with a new and strange thought. The light in the marrefia bet that made darkness bright would shine through the village just as the knowledge they gained would lighten the days ahead.

12

THE WORLD
BECOMES
WIDE

TEFFERA and the other boys sat in a circle on the floor of Mr. Sam Jones's house. As he had said, the light of the lantern made it bright as day.

Each boy had a pencil and paper, like those Teffera had treasured so much. They had not been a special mark of friendship and esteem, as he had thought, but things which the ferangi might give carelessly to anyone.

A new resolve had come to Teffera—to follow the example set by his father. When his father went to the hospital he had made up his mind to accept the gift of sight from the ferangi, if they gave it, but not to become like them in any way. So would he learn all that he could from Mr. Sam Jones, but stand wary and aloof from him, watching for any sign of treachery.

"I'll write your names for you," Mr. Sam Jones said, "and then you can copy them. This is one way you might learn." He took a large sheet of paper and wrote a word on it, then held it up for them to see. Putting the point of his pencil at the spot where he had begun, he retraced the lines he had made. "If you practice going over and over your name first, it will be easier for you to write it by yourself."

As soon as each boy had the pattern of his name he began work. Teffera was amused to see what had happened to him the day before happen with the others. First they approached the task with great confidence, but after a few broken pencil points and many mistakes, they settled down with dogged determination.

The room became very quiet, with only the tight breathing of those who struggled and the sounds of pencils moving on paper disturbing the air. Sometimes a boy would put his paper down in disgust as if he wanted no more of this peculiar task, but when his glance around the room showed everyone else working, he bent to the job again.

"Maybe it will go quicker if I tell you a story while you write," said Mr. Sam Jones. "Would you like to hear 'The Goats who Killed the Leopard?' "

The boys nodded happily. They all knew the story, and liked it.

"Once upon a time," Mr. Sam Jones began, "a large and fierce leopard stalked a herd of goats and began killing them off, one by one. Each day the herd became smaller. Finally, in desperation, one of the goats complained to a friendly monkey to see if he would help.

" 'Go to the leopard,' " he begged, " 'and see why he is so angry with us. We have lived here peaceably for many years and have never wronged him, or even thought evil thoughts about him.' "

"The monkey, who like all of his tribe took a great interest in the business of others, made his way into the jungle until he found the leopard.

" 'I have come as an ambassador,' he said, sounding very important for such a small animal. 'It is my mission to find out from you why you are killing off the herd of goats that lives in the cave by the brook.'

97

"The leopard raised his great head and smiled, showing his evil teeth. 'It is to revenge the honor of my family,' he said piously. 'One of the fierce goats of that tribe killed one of my cousins, and I cannot rest until I have repaid the debt in full.'

"The monkey scratched his round head in perplexity. Goats have many faults, but he had never heard of one attacking such a ferocious beast as a leopard. Besides, he had heard many times how the leopard's cousin had been killed, and the goats had had nothing to do with it.

"'But that was an elephant,' he said. 'Walking through the dark jungle one night, he accidentally stepped on your cousin. Everyone knows about it.'

"The leopard smiled innocently and lowered his eyes. 'What a foolish story!' he said. 'How can the elephant be guilty when he is so much larger than I, and not nearly so good to eat as the goats?' "

The laughter of the boys bubbled up and filled the brightly lighted room. Each time they heard the story it was slightly different, and each time they liked it better.

"Tell us a story from your country," said one of the boys. "What is it like where you live?"

Mr. Sam Jones thought a minute and then got to his feet. "First I'll tell you where my country is," he said. He walked to a table on the side of the room and picked up a book. Turning the pages, he found what he was looking for, and opened the book to show them.

"The world is very large," he said, "and there are many different countries in it. Some of the world is covered with water and some of it is land. Some of the lands are so big they are called continents. Your country is in the continent of Africa, and this is a picture of it."

The boys peered at the strange picture and watched while he pointed out the country of Ethiopia. With his pencil he touched one spot on the map.

"This is just about where we are right now," he said. "And here is your capital, Addis Ababa, where Teffera's father is in the hospital."

Retta laughed. "That cannot be true. Addis Ababa is much farther from us than that."

"And Ethiopia is much bigger than this picture," said Mr. Jones. "Maps must be drawn smaller than the countries they show, or they couldn't be put in books." He turned more pages and showed them another map. "This is the part of the world that contains Africa," he said. "Above it, and to one side, is a large, large continent which contains the European and Asian countries."

"Show us where your home is," said Retta.

"My home isn't on this map. It's on the other side of the world. The world is round, you know, like a ball, and there are two great continents on the other side." He turned the pages again and showed them another map. "The continent at the top is called North America, where I live, and the one at the bottom is called South America."

Teffera felt his head whirling. Often, as he had sat on the hillside watching his sheep he had looked at the sky above him, and then around him as far as he could see. He had thought how big the village was where he lived, with its many fields and meadows and hills and streams. He had thought how huge the sky was, with the sun so far above, and the moon and stars at night. Now Mr. Sam Jones was telling him the world was much bigger than this, so big that he could not even imagine it. What sort of book was this that he showed them, that had such strange pictures and said such unbelievable things?

"When you go to school," Mr. Jones went on, "you will have books like this to read that will tell you about the world."

"Who wrote these books?" asked one of the boys. "Where do they come from? How do we know that they are true?"

Mr. Jones had to think about that for a minute. "Well, I'll tell you," he said. "You know that last week Teffera and his mother had a letter from his father, who is in Addis Ababa. Teffera has never been in Addis Ababa, but he has been in a hospital. The letter told him something he did not know before about the hospital where his father is, and about what is happening. He knows that his father would not tell him a lie, so he can believe what the letter says.

"Teffera and his mother have written Ato Paulos a letter to tell him what he did not know about things that are happening here, and he will believe what their letter says.

"The books you will read when you go to school are like letters from other people to you. Each person who writes a book has something special that he wants to share with others, so he puts it into words that everyone can read.

"Your government is anxious for all of the people of Ethiopia to learn as much as they can. Much money is being spent to build schools and to hire teachers. For many years, those who wished a very good education had to go to other countries to complete their search for knowledge, but now colleges are established here.

"Every school has many books, because books are where the knowledge of the world is stored. You can be sure that your government does not want you to learn from books that you cannot believe."

Teffera had heard this before, because it was one of the strongest arguments his uncle Bekele had used to have him go to school.

"In the past, the people of Ethiopia guarded and protected it by being brave warriors, and now they will guard and protect it by learning all they can. The officials in charge of the schools are working hard to get the best books and the best teachers they can."

Teffera felt a tug at his conscience. If his government knew all about the books that were being used in the schools, and about the teachers, some of whom were ferangis, did it also know about all of the ferangis who came into the country? If the government approved of Mr. Sam Jones, who was he to doubt him?

He thought of that morning on the hillside, and how Mr. Sam Jones and the boys had examined his special flock of sheep and had seen no evidence of what he had done. The ram was muddy, to be sure, but not so much more than any of the others that it had caused any comment.

The dye was so well hidden by the mud that his secret was safe. He had deceived Mr. Sam Jones successfully, but was it wrong to deceive a ferangi? He would not deceive his father or any member of his family, or any of his friends, but were foreigners to be thought of in the same way?

Had God not made them different and strange to show that they were not Ethiopians? Was it necessary, then, to treat them as equals?

13

THE ANGER

OF

RETTA

"Do you think you can handle them?" Mr. Sam Jones asked, handing the shears to Teffera.

The boy nodded and looked at the sheep with dismay. His clever plot was becoming so complicated he began to wonder if he had been so clever, after all. First he had planned to slip the prize ram into the pen with the culls early one morning before anyone else was up. Then he had realized the culls were so thin, and his ram so handsome, Mr. Sam Jones would see the difference at once. That problem had been easy to solve. The culls were to be fattened, and once they were fat he could put his ram among them and only a sharp eye would see the difference.

That solution only led to another difficulty. The sheep in the pen were to be sheared, partly for their health and partly so that Mr. Sam Jones could teach the boys how it was done. Teffera had had no intention of working with the group among whom Mr.

Sam Jones had distributed his favors. A much better plan had entered his mind. He would stay to one side, ignoring the others, and learn what he could by watching and listening through his hole in the barricade. That would be enough to see him through the time that Mr. Sam Jones was here, and next year he would go to school. In school he would learn to read, and once he could read he would find many books about sheep that would tell him everything he needed to know.

But if the sheep in the pen were sheared, how could he slip an unshorn sheep among them and fool anyone? So it was obvious that he must get the ram shorn. And since Mr. Sam Jones had kept to his side of the bargain and had not even suggested doing anything to Teffera's sheep, how would it get done unless he did it himself?

That was how it came about that he found himself laboriously trying to manipulate a tool that seemed very simple in the hands of Mr. Sam Jones and very contrary in his own.

He gritted his teeth and made up his mind he could do as well as anyone else. Like writing his name, he found that it became easier as he worked, and he began to feel a certain satisfaction in learning something new.

As the boys clipped, Mr. Sam Jones talked with them. He encouraged them to tell of the courage of Ethiopian soldiers in their great battles, and he told them about the war America had fought for her freedom.

The boys were fascinated with his tales of the well-trained and regimented British soldiers and the poorly dressed and poorly fed American troops who had finally triumphed. They could understand the way the Americans had fought and the hardships they had endured because they were so akin to what had happened in their own country.

Perhaps, Teffera mused, all ferangis were not alike, perhaps Mr. Sam Jones's people were like the Ethiopians. Even if they looked different and had a different language and were peculiar in many ways, perhaps they were still similar enough to be understood and trusted. Some other ferangis, who had come to Ethiopia pretending to be friendly but acting as enemies, were truly bad, but the Americans meant well, like the Ethiopians.

But Mr. Sam Jones had said this was not so. He had said that in his own country there were many people and that some of them were good and some were bad. There were people of different races, too. He had said that each person must be judged by what he was, and not by his country or his color or his language.

It was all very hard to understand.

Retta dropped his shears in disgust.

"I do not think I like this much," he said. "There are too many new things in our village now. It was better the way it was before."

In the marrefia bet at night, while the other boys worked faithfully, Retta had complained and been lazy. At first he had been sure he could learn to write more quickly than anyone, but when a boy had laughed at the first scraggly letters he made, he had become angry.

"Why must I write just as everyone else does?" he had asked. "I do not look like everyone else, so why must I make the same marks? As a matter of fact, I think my letters are more beautiful the way I make them."

It was true that Retta had made nice marks and he had even drawn pictures with his pencil that the others could recognize. Mr. Sam Jones had complimented him on his drawing, so that he had become proud of himself and had decided that he was too clever to make letters like the others. Page after page of his tablet had been covered with trees and birds and flowers and weapons, and Mr. Sam Jones had not scolded him but had praised him.

"Perhaps Retta is to be an artist," he had said, and had told them of the beautiful paintings in the great churches of Ethiopia.

Now Retta was bored with shearing the sheep and wanted to do something else.

"When they are all shorn they will have to be sprayed," Mr. Sam Jones said. "Maybe you will enjoy that more."

Retta wrinkled his nose. "The spray smells bad. I think I will sit here for a while and watch the others."

"You could lead us in a song," suggested Mr. Jones. "I'd like to learn some of your songs so I can teach them to my son."

This kept Retta happy for a while, and he was even interested in learning one of Mr. Sam Jones's songs and singing it with the others. Privately, Teffera did not think the ferangi song sounded like music, but it seemed pleasanter as he heard it repeated.

The next day Retta did not come to work with the boys, nor did he come to the marrefia bet at night. The next day he appeared for a little while, but only to watch the others and make sly remarks about their awkwardness.

Teffera was worried, because he knew that once Retta's enmity was aroused he did not forget easily, and was capable of much mischief.

"You do not need to learn to care for sheep," he said one morning, when Retta was more troublesome than ever. "When you are grown you will raise teff, just as your father does, and this knowledge will not help you. I wish you would come at night when we study, though, because what we learn will be useful when the school is built in the village."

"What school?" asked Retta, innocently. "Who says we are to have a school? Our village is so poor perhaps we cannot build one. My father says that schools teach good Ethiopians to be beasts."

"Are we learning to be beasts in the marrefia bet?" asked Teffera. "Has it hurt any of us to learn to write our names? Are we not doing things to make our fathers proud of us?"

Teffera had a special reason for being contented with his studies. Because he had learned to write his name so quickly, and without any help, Mr. Sam Jones had given him something very exciting to do. Mr. Sam Jones had written a letter for him to his

father, and now Teffera was copying it, word by word, with his own hand. When it was completed he would mail it to his father in the hospital, and he knew that it would be received with love and pride.

"It is all tricks," murmured Retta. "We have let the ferangi come into the village and lead us about as if we were your own silly sheep. When he has us completely in his power, he will strike. As for me, I will have nothing more to do with it. Then, when the danger comes, I will be safe. But you may call on me for help, because I am still your friend, whatever happens."

This lifted a load from Teffera's heart. Retta had been his friend since they were small, and he did not want the new ways or the new learning to come between them. He remembered how he had felt to see how his uncle Bekele lived, and could understand how Retta felt.

Besides, Retta had always liked to play games in which he was the leader, and had always wanted to be looked up to by everyone. His troubles with writing, and his lack of interest in the sheep, were probably all that bothered him. He would recover before too long and all would be as it was.

He did not like what Retta had said about the school, since it might be an echo of what the village was saying. Although Teffera still did not want to go to the town and live with his uncle Bekele and go to school, he did want more than anything to go to school in his own village. The books written to him as letters from the world seemed to be all he could think of these days.

With all of this knowledge at his command, there was no limit to what brave deeds he might do for his country!

14

THE FEAST OF THE FINDING

OF THE

TRUE CROSS

As the days of the month of Maskaram passed, the fields and meadows turned to gold. The millions of yellow flowers blooming as far as the eye could see seemed to be telling Teffera that the world was good, that God's eye was on His children.

The spirits of Mr. Sam Jones became even more cheerful than usual. "Our culls are getting fatter," he said, "and when we're ready to butcher, we'll invite the whole village in to watch. If there are still any doubts in their minds, that should settle them."

His words brought the old worries back to Teffera. He hoped that Mr. Sam Jones was right, but he had not seen Retta lately and he did not know what people were saying now about the ferangi.

He had personally checked the sheep in the pen, and had compared them to his ram, and he knew that the time had come to finish his big plan. Very early in the morning, as soon as it was light enough for him to see, he would shear the ram and put it in the pen with the other sheep. He would do a rough, uneven job, so that no one could see it had been shorn so recently, and then it would not be recognized for what it was.

He still had doubts about what he was doing, but something told him he was right. If Mr. Sam Jones meant no evil, his work would not be harmed. If he did, it was best that he be exposed.

The shearing and the substitution were much easier than he had expected. It was almost as if God were showing that He was pleased with what Teffera had in mind. The night shepherd was pleased to leave his post early and Mr. Sam Jones did not come out into the field until an hour after the ram had been slipped in with the culls.

Looking over the sheep in the pen, Teffera realized that the culls, which had been poor and miserable before, were now so fat and sleek it was almost unbelievable. His own prize ram hardly looked different, except to the expert eye. Mr. Sam Jones had such an eye, so no mistake was possible.

Although no one was there to see him, he put a confident smile on his lips to hide his inner qualms. He had not meant to do wrong, and so what he did could not be wrong. Besides, it was the time of Mascal, when God was very close to Ethiopia, and His spirit would surely make everything right. As they celebrated the finding of the True Cross, he would pray that Mr. Sam Jones was as good as he seemed and had no wish to kill a good ram. His conscience reminded him that he had also better pray that the ferangi not be allowed to make an innocent mistake.

In the early evening the boys of the village gathered to go into the woods and cut their poles for the Mascal celebration. Retta was with them, but he did not talk as freely to Teffera as he usually did. He was not cold, but aloof, as if his mind were on other things. If he had mischievous plans or evil thoughts, he did not confide them to Teffera.

All of the village made ready for Mascal, which was to be celebrated in the large flat meadow a few miles away. Everyone prepared his finest clothes, and each shemma was washed until it gleamed in whiteness. Teffera's mother sang as she went about her work, happy with the news from Paulos. The bandages were soon to be removed from his eyes, and the doctors were sure that he would be completely cured.

On the morning of Mascal, Teffera's mother joined with the other women of the village as they began their walk to the field. All of the men and boys, carrying their tall poles topped with bunches of the golden flowers of Maskaram, went together, led by the elders. The procession was happy but solemn, each heart filled with the joy of the festival.

The beautiful but sad voices of the women rose through the clear air to the very gates of heaven, carrying praise to God. People from other villages joined them, many people on horseback, and all of them singing and humming as they went.

In the center of the meadow was a tall pole, the Demarra, its tip almost as high as the eye could reach, and covered with a cloth of many colors. To the left of the pole stood the priests and deacons, splendid in their brilliant robes, and to the right were the officials and elders of the whole area. Teffera and the other worshipers took their places to make a circle around the Demarra. All became quiet as the priests began their chanting, and even the happy children were silent in the glory of the moment.

When the chanting of the priests was through, the measured and stately dance began, each prince of the church expressing his devotion to God as David had shown it when he danced before the Ark. Three times the beautiful procession circled the Demarra, and the last time the priests and deacons cast their tokens of golden flowers at the foot of the tall pole.

Teffera joined in the procession with the others, his voice raised in song, and laid his own pole with theirs to surround the Demarra. There was so much joy and gladness in the air it seemed as if his heart would burst with it. The gleaming white shemmas of his beloved people seemed to twinkle in the brilliant

warm sun above the golden earth like stars or heavenly flowers bending and swaying in the air.

All through the day the rejoicing continued, each heart glad that God had shown his pleasure in His beloved people by giving them the gift of the True Cross. In the evening, when the sun had gone to rest and the evening shadows lengthened on the meadow, the Demarra and its golden flowers were set on fire, the flames dancing upward to the very throne of God. Teffera stayed with the others to watch, dancing and singing until his joy knew no bounds.

It was late at night when they returned to their village, and very early in the morning they returned to the Demarra. As Teffera took ashes from the remains of the fire to mark the Cross on his forehead, he said a very special prayer in his heart.

Even though Mr. Jones had disappointed him in some ways, he had come to like and respect him. He was not like a father, nor yet like a priest, nor yet like a doctor, but he had done something for Teffera that none of these had done. What he had taught in his lighted marrefia bet in the evenings had been little, as he had said, but it had opened windows in Teffera's mind through which he could see the limitless world in which he lived. As his fingers traced the outline of the Cross on his forehead, he prayed that Mr. Sam Jones would pass the test that he had set for him, and that all would be well with him and with the village.

The very next morning Mr. Sam Jones received a message as soon as they returned to the village. Retta came to deliver it, smiling and excited with his importance. He handed the letter to the ferangi and waited while he opened it.

"I have to go into town for a few days," the ferangi said after he read it. "Some government officials will be there, and they want to talk to me. Teffera, do you think you can take over while I'm gone?" Quickly he gave directions, explaining again all that they had been doing.

"I don't think any of the sheep will have to be sprayed again, but keep a sharp eye out for ticks. And be sure the culls get the extra feed we've been giving them, because we'll want to butcher right after I get back. I think all of you understand pretty well what to do, and I won't worry a bit while I'm gone. Okay?"

Teffera knew this American word very well. He felt proud of the trust imposed on him, and sure that he would earn it. "Ishi," he said.

He could not help a small measure of sadness as he saw the ferangi drive off in his now familiar car, but it was only for a while. Soon he would be back, and the lessons in the marrefia bet would begin again.

Everything went well for the rest of the morning, but in the afternoon he looked up and saw a number of men approaching, Retta leading the way. The air of the men was not pleasant, and they were talking excitedly among themselves.

"I can show you what he is doing," Retta was saying. "I looked again at the sheep yesterday, and it is all a trick. Come with me, and I will show you."

The boys who had been helping did not like this any more than Teffera. One by one they slipped off to stand on the sidelines, leaving Teffera alone to face them.

Retta walked boldly up to the pen and opened the door for the men to walk in after him. "See these sheep," he said, "and how fat they are. The ferangi pretends that they are culls, the sick ones that should be killed. Their fleece is gone so you can see the fat on their ribs. Do they look sick to you?"

The men examined the sheep, and Teffera, with horror, saw that one of them was checking his prize ram over carefully. When the man had finished, he spoke. "I will take my oath that there is no finer sheep than this one in the entire herd."

"That is what he has done," said Retta. "First he put the poor, thin sheep in here, and then, when we were not watching, he exchanged the good ones for them. Look at those outside the pen, and you will see that they are not nearly so fat as these."

Teffera knew that this was true. Mr. Sam Jones had told him that it was not good for breeding sheep to become too fat, or else the lambs would suffer. The sheep inside the pen had been given much extra food so they would become very fat and heavy.

He wanted to tell them, but he could not. With Mr. Sam Jones he could now talk easily and freely, because that was what the ferangi expected, but these men were different. They were elders of his village and would be furious if he tried to correct them, and besides, they looked very sullen and angry. Not all of the men were there, he saw only a dozen or so, and most of them the special friends of Retta's father.

Suddenly he remembered the story of the goats that killed the leopard. Mr. Sam Jones had not harmed Retta, or the other men, but Retta's feelings had been hurt. Because he had been lazy and uninterested he had become angry. He had picked Mr. Sam Jones as his enemy, when it was his own lazy nature that had kept him from being superior to all of the others. His anger had turned against the ferangi, and he had influenced his father and the other men. All of this was too hard to explain, and Teffera knew it could never be done.

Now the village would turn on Mr. Sam Jones, who was innocent, and ruin everything that he had tried to do for the village.

"Shall we destroy the ferangi's marrefia bet, and run him out of town when he returns?" asked a hothead from the group.

Retta's father looked uneasy. He liked excitement and turmoil, but had never caused any real trouble.

"No, it may be that our government wanted him to come," he said. "I think we must first prove that he is doing wrong. When does he plan to butcher these sheep?" he asked.

Retta shook his head because he did not know, and none of the other boys spoke up, so Teffera stepped forward.

"He will do it when he comes back, and he will invite the

whole village to see," he said. Then a daring thought came to him. Could he stake everything on his belief that Mr. Sam Jones meant only good? Rapidly he went back over everything that he knew of him, everything he had done in the time he had been in the village. Except for not understanding all of their customs, and making Teffera jealous by forgetting their special friendship, he had done nothing wrong. And perhaps he had not meant wrong by those things, if you remembered that he was from a different country. Yes, he would risk it!

"May I say something to you?" he asked. "It is a long story, but I hope you will listen."

The men agreed, obviously more than willing to find some way of handling the problem which would not bring trouble upon them.

Teffera told them of how he had built the barricade and hidden his best sheep behind it, and how Mr. Sam Jones had discovered what he had done. Some of the men nodded in praise for his cleverness. Then he told of Mr. Sam Jones's decision to use the two groups of sheep as a test of which way of caring for them was best, and that, too, seemed good to the men.

He told of his new doubts, and of the great trick he had played, and how he had marked the prize ram as a test for the ferangi. Going into the pen, he found the ram and brought it out so they could all see it. He showed them the dye mark on its chest which proved that it was this ram, and no other.

"Retta has told you that the sheep in the pen are fatter and healthier than those in the pasture, and this is partly true and partly false. The penned sheep are fatter because we have been feeding them to make them fat. The others are leaner because Mr. Sam Jones says that is better for them. If you will look closely and feel their flesh, you can tell these sheep have thin, narrow bones, and that is why the ferangi says they should be butchered. But my ram is not like that—he is broad and stocky and strong.

"Not everyone could see the difference, but Mr. Sam Jones

knows sheep as a mother knows her baby, and he can tell that this ram should not be butchered. So that is my test for him. If he truly wants to help us, he will discover that the ram does not belong here. If he has been tricking us, he will be glad to slaughter the good ram with the others, and will think that an accident has brought him good luck."

The men nodded approvingly and began to talk among themselves. Finally Retta's father spoke.

"You have been very wise, Teffera. When your father learns what you have done he will be proud of you. All that we need to do now is wait and see what happens. If the ferangi falls into your trap, all that Retta has said may be true. If he does not, then what you have said is true. If Retta has been wrong, it may be that he will suffer for it."

15

THE FERANGI

IS

TESTED

TEFFERA carried out his duties faithfully in the next few days, and the other boys helped him, but he was miserable and unhappy. Had he betrayed one who only befriended him, or had he set a trap to save his village from trouble?

What if Mr. Sam Jones was really good, but made a mistake when he checked the sheep? What if he never checked them at all, but went on with the slaughter, since he had no reason to suspect that they were anything but culls?

On the day the ferangi returned, Teffera found it hard to greet him and smile as he always had. What Mr. Sam Jones told him made it worse.

"I phoned the hospital while I was in town, and talked to your father on the telephone. He sends his love to all of you and says to tell you that he should be home in a week or two. The bandages are off his eyes now, and he has to wear dark glasses for a while, but the doctors think he's cured. I told him you had a surprise for him, Teffera, but I didn't tell him what it was."

Teffera had finished the letter now, but he could hardly bring himself to show it to the ferangi and ask him to mail it. If he had betrayed him, how could he ask him for more favors?

"And I got something for Retta, too," Mr. Sam Jones went on. "He quit coming to our lessons because someone laughed at the way he wrote, and I've felt badly about that. Retta's a bright boy, and a lot of people have trouble when they first learn to write. I thought this might cheer him up, and give him a chance to do something he's really good at, so he'd be encouraged to keep on."

He opened the flat box and showed Teffera the blocks of color and the brushes it contained. "He's really good at drawing, and I thought he might like to try painting, too. I got him a pad of the right kind of paper. Do you think he'll like it?"

A surge of bitter happiness arose in Teffera's breast. At least, he would now have someone to share his own sense of guilt and shame. "I will go and get him," he said. "I will be glad to."

He found Retta sitting outside his own house, looking bored and miserable. It could not have been easy for him, who was usually the center of the group, to stay away from the others because he did not like what they were doing.

"I have brought you good news," Teffera said, hiding his emotion. "The ferangi has returned, and he wishes to see you because he thinks so well of you. He has been worried about you because you did not come to lessons, and he was afraid you felt badly because someone laughed at your writing. He thought that was very bad, because he admired you very much, and is eager for you to learn. He thinks that you have great talent and will grow up to be a wise man, and he wishes to help you."

Retta tried to keep his face blank, but he understood every word that Teffera was not saying, and every emotion that he was not showing. He twisted to one side and hung his head. Perhaps he, too, remembered the excitement and warmth of the evenings in the marrefia bet. "Tell him I thank him very much, and that I, too, wish him well," he said.

Teffera made his voice cold. "That is not enough. The ferangi has brought you a gift, which he wishes to give you in person. He says that our village has been so kind to him that he would like to repay our kindness in every way he can. Have we not, after all, allowed him to work every day with the sheep, and to teach us every evening in his house? Is it not wonderful that we have done so much for one who is not even of our own blood, but a stranger?"

Retta's face softened and he looked at Teffera with the old eyes of friendship. "You are hurt, too, Teffera, or you would not talk so. All right, I did mischief, and I know it. I have thought it all over, and I believe that I was wrong, and I am sorry I said things that were not true. I will go with you to the ferangi, and tell him, and say that I am sorry."

Teffera put out his hand and Retta clenched it in his. "I wish that you could," he said, "but you must not. Your guilt is not as bad as mine, and he must not know yet about mine. It is I who have laid the trap for him, and I have told the village about it, and I cannot be false to them. The ferangi is a good man, but this is our home, and these are our people, and we must love our own country best."

Together the boys went to Mr. Sam Jones, and when Retta saw the gift for him he was not able to speak for a long time. "Someday I will be worthy of your gift," he said slowly.

Mr. Sam Jones squeezed his shoulder affectionately. "You're worthy of it now," he said. "You boys have been wonderful, and I've enjoyed every minute of being here. I thought you'd like the paints, and I have a book on sheep for Teffera. Now if you'd like to do something this minute to help me, go and tell the people in the village that we'll butcher the sheep tomorrow. I found out in town that I have to leave right away for the capital, so we'll have to move faster than I thought. Will you do that?"

120

The boys rushed off, eager to go and be away from his kindly face and warm voice and be busy at something that would keep them from thinking. It was late when they had visited the last house in the village with their message, but tired as he was, Teffera found it difficult to go to sleep.

The next morning almost everyone in the village was on the hillside to see the sheep and watch the ferangi take his test. They were smiling and courteous as always, so the ferangi could not tell what they were thinking, and opinion seemed to be divided evenly among them.

They could see that the sheep cared for by Mr. Sam Jones looked well, and it seemed to Teffera that they looked better than the ones he had hidden behind the barricade for protection.

The ferangi explained all of the things he had done, and showed them the equipment he had used.

"The boys who helped me know all about it, and they can do everything I have done. You should be very proud of them, because they learn quickly."

He led them to the pen. "These are the culls of the flock, the ones we picked out as the worst. If they were kept they would have poor lambs, and the flock as a whole would not improve. We didn't want to waste them, though, so we've been fattening them up so they'll make better eating. If you'll come in here with me, I'll show you why we selected them, and why they're still poor sheep even if they're fat."

He got on his knees and showed one of the men how to check the sheep, feeling the bones and seeing how its legs were set closely together.

A feeling of tension had settled over the crowd. They all knew, because news travels fast in a village, what Teffera had done. Would the ferangi pass his test or not? Doubtful looks were on some of the faces. They had watched the stranger for weeks, had talked to him, and had seen how he had taught their sons. Was this fair to him, was it a kind way to treat one who had shown them only a friendly face?

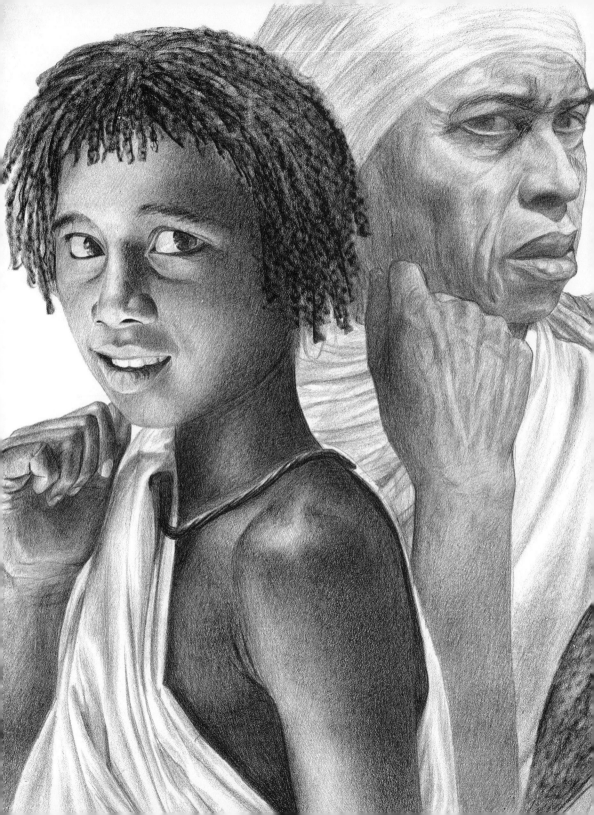

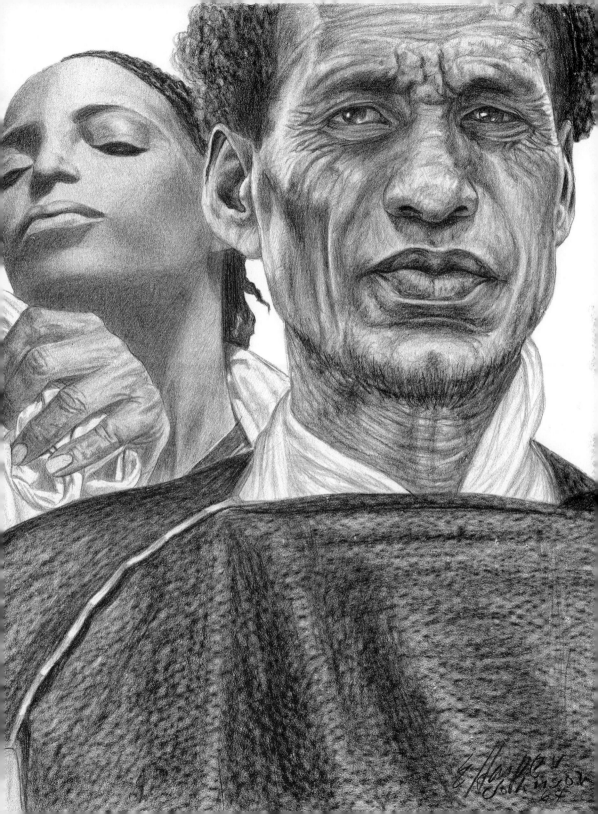

The moment was growing closer. Mr. Sam Jones had shown them how they selected the culls, and now it was time for the butchering to begin. Would his clever eye light on the prize ram among the culls, or would he even notice it? Had he already seen it, and known that this was his chance to destroy the best ram of the entire flock without anyone suspecting?

More than the fate of the ram was in the balance. If the ferangi showed himself to be evil, no one would have any trust in anything he had taught, or in any of the new ways. The village would not want a school where their sons might learn wickedness and dishonesty and destruction to the things they held dear.

Mr. Sam Jones got to his feet again and opened his mouth to speak. Just then Retta's father stepped forward. "I do not raise sheep," he said, "but I find this very interesting. You have said that these sheep to be butchered are poorer than the others, but they look fatter to me. I still do not understand why you say this."

"Why, sure. Come here and I'll show you. Feel this sheep, and see how small his bones are."

Retta's father did as he was told, a look of great concentration on his face. When he was finished, he nodded doubtfully. "I think I understand," he said, "but could we try again on a different sheep? Some of the others look even better than this one."

"Sure." They moved a few feet and stopped by another one and again the process was repeated. Those who were watching began to frown in bewilderment. Why was Retta's father suddenly so interested in sheep, and why was he pretending to be so stupid?

Again he acted puzzled and he and the ferangi singled out another sheep. Suspicion gathered in Teffera's mind, but it was hard to believe.

"Now!" said Retta's father suddenly. "I think I have it." All of the time his eyes were scanning the sheep, comparing one to another. "If the legs grow too closely together, and if the bones

124

are thin, then the sheep is not good. Is that right?"

Mr. Sam Jones nodded happily. "That's it," he said. "It's really quite simple."

The eyes of Retta's father lighted on a certain ram and a broad smile covered his face.

"Then this one I will test for myself," he said, and began to feel of its bones. Slowly, dramatically, his expression changed and he began to shake his head.

"I am afraid I do not understand after all." His voice sounded uncertain. "I do not feel the bones properly."

Mr. Sam Jones went over to him. "Here, let me," he said. After a minute, he, too, looked puzzled and began giving the sheep a thorough examination.

"Well, this is either the first miracle I ever saw, or there's been a mistake," he said. "This isn't a cull. It's the best ram in the whole herd."

A sudden and hilarious shriek of laughter went up from the group, as if they had been released from an unbearable tension. Now they saw what Retta's father had been doing! He had made absolutely sure that Mr. Sam Jones examined the good ram for himself so that his intentions were quite clear. It might easily have escaped his eye, in the excitement, and have been butchered with the rest, so that no one would have known for sure whether or not it was a mistake.

They crowded around the ferangi, shaking his hand and smiling at him. Retta's father smiled proudly at his own cleverness. The ferangi was too pleased with their happiness to ask questions at the moment, but Teffera saw a bewildered look on his face before he was swallowed up by the crowd.

"Tomorrow we will give a feast for the ferangi," said Retta's father, and everyone chorused agreement. "It was a good day when he came to our village."

Teffera knew that Retta must have talked to his father to make him change his mind, and he was proud of his friend. He was proud of his village for their joy that the ferangi had proved himself to be good and he knew that they would have felt sorrow as well as anger if Mr. Sam Jones had failed to pass his test. There was no one of whom he not was proud, except himself. He knew what he would have to do, but he wondered if he could find the courage to do it.

Mr. Sam Jones could not be expected to forgive him, nor could Teffera blame him for that. Everything that the stranger had done was now clear, and it seemed mean and small for Teffera to have doubted him. The ferangi had come to their village with only friendliness in his heart, he had worked long hours to teach and help them, and had been especially thoughtful with Teffera and his family. The doubt and mistrust with which he had been repaid was enough to make him hate Teffera forever.

The afternoon shadows began to fall on the grass as he mused, and his heart hung heavy in his breast, weighed down with sorrow. Soon he would have to go to the marrefia bet and tell Mr. Sam Jones the truth, because it was not honest to hide what he had done. He would also return the tablets and the pencils and even the paper with his name written on it. It was not right to keep gifts from one you had wronged. He sighed deeply and wondered if there was a boy in Ethiopia, or even in the whole world, as unhappy as he.

A sudden sound caught his attention and he jerked his head upright, his eyes wide open. The moment could no longer be averted. Mr. Sam Jones was before him. He opened his mouth, but the ferangi spoke first. "Retta told me what you did," he said, "and I want to tell you that I admire you, Teffera."

Teffera did not believe his ears. This was a dream, in which his unhappy mind had sought solace because it did not want to face the truth.

"Life is difficult in your country now, Teffera, because so many things are changing, and you do not know what to believe. It would be wrong for your people to shut their eyes to the out-

side world and to refuse to have anything to do with the new knowledge and ideas, but it would be equally bad if they tried to be like the rest of the world.

"I do not think you tried to trick me because you disliked me, but only to be sure that I was not bringing harm to your village."

Teffera took the hand Mr. Sam Jones held out, trying to put all of his relief and pride and affection into the gesture.

"Then you do not think the Ethiopians should change and be like the ferangis?"

Mr. Sam Jones laughed. "Certainly not. Your country is very old and very proud, and different from any other country in the world. I hope it will grow and become stronger, but always remain itself."

Teffera thought of the gifts that the ferangi had brought to the village, and knew that this was the best of all. He had not wanted to change the sheep, but to improve them, and had not even wanted Retta to change, but to learn to use his special gifts in his own way.

"We will miss you when you are gone," he said.

"And I will miss you, too, Teffera. But tell me, what will you do when I am gone?"

Teffera raised his head and looked around him, at the wall he had built of thornbush to save his precious sheep from destruction.

"First I will go inside the barricade, and I will shear all of the sheep and spray them. Then I will cut down the thornbush and burn it, and put all of the sheep back together again."

Mr. Sam Jones looked at him and their eyes met in a smile. "Cut down the cantuffa," the ferangi quoted, "in the four quarters of the world . . ."

Teffera laughed. "But I know where I am going," he said.

128